Maki

J. Manque

fiction

Where they burn books, ultimately they burn bodies—
Heinrich Heine

For Sheena

—whose fearless deeds prick authoritarian death cults
& death alike—

preface

When I wrote this story I never planned on publishing it. It was a personal response to what I pessimistically see as a culture reverting to the most destructive forms of tribalism, orchestrated by the powerful as a way of cementing their control by appealing to the base instincts of their followers instead of encouraging them to follow their better angels, the cultural equivalent of schoolyard monitors shoving the youngest kids on the playground together and chanting, "Fight, fight, fight," when nobody's looking—but everyone is looking, and nobody cares. I normally don't write horror, and certainly nothing akin to body horror, but this was a way to vent my outrage, the literary equivalent of screaming into the wilderness, a way to clear my head for more serious efforts, and as an experiment in pushing recursive and disjointed storytelling, intentionally overwrought in places to mirror our innermost thoughts when we're in pain.

I told a friend I'd written it, and why. To my surprise she asked if she could see it, and though she compared reading it to electrocution —once she grabbed the wire she couldn't let go— she did tell me she thought others should be able to experience it as well. As I respect her opinion I've decided to make it available with only mild trepidation, and with apologies in advance if I disgust anyone.

Be warned, this story is about monsters. It's about monsters whose reflections we might catch in a mirror. It's about monsters that think changing things is more important than how they're changed. It's about monsters that think tearing down the old is all there is to building the new. It's about monsters that think they're making a difference, and monsters that think are the scariest kind of all.

J. Manque, March 31th, 2024

Part I

After decades of unrest and anger that seemed to play out entirely on the omnipresent screens that define our culture, our politicians, in concert with the thinkers, teachers, entrepreneurs, activists, and other stakeholders, came to the conclusion that if things continued on their current trajectory our society would disintegrate, that it was diseased with an aggressive cancer that needed to be cut away before it spread, that we needed new ideas, and entirely new ways of doing things. It was time to grab the gently wavering needle of the moral compass, force it to point towards 'good' and weld it there—forever. Accepting division as part of normal social intercourse was an error to be consigned to the ash heap of history, especially when those who disagreed with them did so strongly, and were so clearly wrong, beyond wrong, even, and the only thing found beyond wrong is evil. They believed half our populace had devolved into something ugly, destructive, reprehensible, something intent on grabbing them and dragging them back, destroying a culture that never actually was, and it's extraordinary the lengths people will go to, to defend something that only ever existed as an ideal, or more precisely, a nostalgic idea. Their first instinct was mass education, but they found that even when they seized virtually all channels of communication that the half of the people who agreed with them didn't need their preaching, and the half who didn't wouldn't even admit to their own ignorance, let alone change their minds and show proper deference to their superior intellect. Next came mandatory deprogramming for the ringleaders, but this was entered into with more zeal than forethought. It proved worse than education. So devious were the degenerates that the number of people successfully deprogrammed was only slightly higher than the number of deprogrammers who ended up switching beliefs and themselves needing deprogramming.

Throughout the discussions of the best way to save the world voices would rise and say, 'We need to consider rounding them all up,' then, 'We may have to round them all up,' followed by the more concise, 'Let's round them all up.' Those voices never specified what was to be done with them after they were collected, either because they never thought beyond the raids and delightful visions of their horrible neighbors with their horrible vehicles with their horrible bumper stickers parked in front of their horrible houses with their horrible flags and their horrible yard signs being led away in handcuffs by people in uniforms with guns, leaving decent people free from their degenerate influences, or because they didn't dare voice what they envisioned, lest it prove more extreme than the others who were thinking the same things, but also self-censoring themselves.

As it turns out they were all pretty much on the same page all along, and consensus was easy to reach, which led to criminal justice reforms that vastly simplified existing law. In fact, they were so simple there was only one sentence for those accused of endangering, or potentially endangering, society or societal norms, truths or potential truths, by any action or inaction, or perceptions thereof—permanent and irrevocable removal from society.

When the reforms were enacted roughly half the country's citizens were sent letters informing them they were under investigation and arrest was possible. Attending the wrong protest, wearing a disruptive color, flying an inappropriate flag, or appropriate flag in the wrong way, saying the wrong thing on social media, saying the right thing at the wrong time, saying anything after getting one of those letters, or having someone whisper you'd done any of those things, was enough to get a special police team to come through your window in the dead of night, or tackle you from behind while walking your kids to school. There was some disagreement whether those letters were meant to scare the creeping indecorous element into compliance and silence, and so avoid having to use the justice system, or whether they were a demonstration of power, sadistically letting people know they would be arrested and removed and were powerless to stop it. Either way, thousands were arrested, every week, thousands that they'd admit to, but it's a big country with a lot of wrongdoers to bring to justice who'd for whole lifetimes hidden behind claims of civil rights to sow seeds of discord to destroy our fragile and precious society; that's the new truth, anyway. The rumors were that there were many, many more arrests than they'd admit to, and that they were taking place at exponentially accelerating rates as the mechanics of the reforms were perfected.

I never received such a letter.

I still don't know why I was arrested, but the whole incident took only seconds, yet it's so vividly etched in my neurons I know I'll never forget it. I was walking through an upscale shopping center on my way to its overpriced supermarket, someplace I went when I only needed a few things because I'm not made of money, just the standard flesh and bone, but it was close enough that I didn't have to get in the car every time I needed milk, at least if it was after payday. I was passing the center's equally upscale exercise studio, its blackened windows offering discounts on the hottest hot yoga classes in town in pink and green temporary paint, when its door slammed open in front of me with a glass shaking rattle that made me jump and stop short, and a woman careened out sideways wearing nothing but a shiny electric blue leotard with yellow piping and a moderately large sweat streak down its front. It probably cost more than my entire ensemble, which, if I'm honest, didn't cost all that much. Its owner was a little pixie MILF in her natural habitat, with radiant salon highlighted blonde hair and shapely, but slightly heavy legs, made to look longer by oblong leg holes cut nearly pelvis high at their peaks. They had a fresh coat of spray-on tan, and were so saturated with scented body oil it made them nearly teak dark and gleam, even in the shade. She would have fallen off the walkway and into the parking lot had she not hit the redwood awning support hard enough to bounce off it, keeping her balance with a few ungainly hops that should have sent her arms spinning to counterbalance, but didn't. She just held them awkwardly behind her, her sweat covered face frozen with the strangest look on it— cornflower blue eyes open wide, mouth half open with bleached teeth gleaming like little pearls surrounded by glossed, but not colored, lips, as befits a woman of a certain age and status exercising in the late morning somewhere her peers might see her.

I can't say I saw fear, elation, or any emotion in that face. I can only describe it as agitated, but the form of agitation eluded me. It took her just a moment to regain her balance, and still jiggling from the original impact, she began running towards me without a word, her bare feet slipping once or twice on the smooth paving before

5

gaining traction, but allowing her to show a rather impressive turn of speed for such a short woman when they did. She brushed me as she went by, and as I turned my head to follow the action I saw the gleam of silver from the handcuffs pinioning her dark wrists behind her which made her not even half dressed bid for freedom, and feats of balance and acceleration, either more impressive or more undignified, but it did send my adrenaline surging, as did the unnerving sight of the police officer coming the other way from behind me, already off his feet to make a diving tackle, but he wasn't headed for her—he was headed for me, and as he made contact and I started to go down I saw the other cop who must have followed her out of the studio, rage written large on his face, lunging for her. I think I probably hit the pavement a second before she did judging by the pathetic mouse-like squeak she made when two hundred twenty pounds of flexing muscle landed on her rather soft hundred pound frame. My head was shoved hard into the cold walkway and I was roughly handcuffed and held down while his comrade dealt with the woman.

He'd yanked her to her feet by her fleshy upper arms. She wasn't dressed for contact sports, especially one played on concrete, and the front of her leotard was abraded and dirty and pulled off one shoulder. One of her thighs and one of her knees were scraped and bloody, but she still tried to dash away again. This time her captor had an arm around her, and though she squirmed like a slippery fish in a grizzly's grasp, like a

6

slippery fish in a grizzly's grasp she couldn't get free. I think she knew she was fighting for her life, and as he leaned back and yanked her off her feet, that she'd lost. In desperation she looked at me, and even though I was as handcuffed as she, and had a knee on my back, an elbow on my head, she demanded hoarsely, "Call my lawyer. Call my lawyer," as she thrashed. There was a brief flash of terror in her eyes as she saw the stun gun come around and its electrodes were jabbed against the bottom of the sweat streak just below her sternum with all the subtly of a combat knife. She tried to say something else, but the device silenced her. She vibrated for a moment, then stiffened as her body was transformed from frightened woman to high voltage electrical conductor. The cop kept the current flowing for the longest time, until it looked like he was holding a mannequin, a wide eyed, sweating, bleeding mannequin. When he finally deactivated the weapon she fell rag doll limp in his arms.

With her neutralized my cop pulled me to my feet with barely more effort than his partner had exerted on the pixie, who had been slung over his shoulder and was carried ahead of me to what I'd assumed was a delivery van parked in the fire lane just a few steps away, but turned out to be an unmarked prisoner shuttle. Several people were filming it with their phones to post online—the geolocations of those phones were known, and for bystanders not to have done so was to suggest disapproval and invite arrest themselves.

7

The inside of the van was divided into six or eight phone booth sized cells. I watched as the woman was thrown into one of them like a sack of potatoes, and the sound of her crumpling as she collapsed to the metal floor was sickening. Then I was shoved in mine hard, and the thick, slit window door slammed shut behind me. I didn't hear the little leotard MILF move or make a sound during the entire ride to the massive new detention center at the edge of town, and I thought she was probably dead, that the electrodes had been too close to her heart and stopped it, but knowing what was likely to happen that may have been a blessing.

And I still can't figure out why that cop was diving for me and not her, not that she appeared to be much of a threat, either. He couldn't have thought I was trying to interfere. From his perspective all he could have seen was me walking then stopping short as the door ahead of me opened. I'd like to think I was just bycatch as they opened their nets for the sweating pixie, because if that's the case then there's an infinitesimal chance someone who matters will actually watch one of the videos the gawkers recorded and realize I didn't do anything before it's too late, but if they were there for me, too, and our proximity just a lucky coincidence for them, then, well, it doesn't bode well for me, not at all. The only thing I was ever told was that I had been arrested for violating the special societal protection section of the new reforms, but everyone is told that when they're taken because it's the only offense codified therein. And if they did come for me I don't know why. Even before the reforms I tried to live a quiet life without conflict, without politics, without opinions ever spoken aloud let alone committed to some reproducible evidentiary form.

I always had my phone in case I were to be in the area of an arrest, disturbance, or public speaker, all of which would have required the same response as those who recorded our arrests. I'd practiced whipping it out and getting it to record within seconds. We all did. Nobody wanted to be the last one recording if someone started screaming about long waits at emergency rooms, the price of energy, centralized thermostat control, food shortages, mandatory injections, or anything else that suggested discontent and needed to be documented so the software monitoring social media could identify miscreants. I wouldn't have wanted to have filmed any of it, but I would have gone through the motions to protect myself. Perhaps by the way I moved when I practiced, or didn't move, the interconnected AI incorporated into everything by mandate was able to detect a lack of enthusiasm that determined I was one of 'them,' or a sympathizer, or a potential convert, or maybe I walked by a security camera at the wrong time a month ago, or eight years ago.

Never let it be said that the reforms eliminated our most basic civil liberties, like a jury trial, though they were streamlined to prevent manipulation by clever lawyers and upstart activists. Defendants were assigned council from a pool of qualified candidates, paid by the state to keep richer clients from getting better representation than poorer, or anyone from getting too much defense. Juries were reduced from twelve to five. Deliberations were deprecated in favor of a single post closing argument vote by show of hands from the jury box with outcomes determined by simple majority, and because of the number of trials the reforms generated it was decided that jurors would have to be full time professionals who also worked for the state, but like defense attorneys, did so independently and without bias. Judges were, however, required to admonish them immediately before their vote that acquittal of a sympathetic, but technically guilty, defendant through jury nullification was itself considered a violation of the reforms and would result in their prosecution, eliminating the shenanigans and tomfoolery pre-reform juries were sometimes known to engage in when they could act without proper oversight, so it was all for the good.

My trial was held about three weeks after my arrest. I wasn't there. My lawyer was, by video. For mutual convenience they conducted twelve trials that day for defendants he was representing. Each of us got half an hour. When we spoke a few days later by phone he didn't remember mine exactly, but thinks it was one of the last of the day—not to worry, though, because we all got the standard defense, which he says is a good one that everyone gets, and we all got the standard conviction and sentence, but that shouldn't be a surprise because he's never heard of a defendant getting

10

acquitted under the new system. One in a thousand, he said, gets a reversal on appeal, and he'd seen two or three of his clients get those, but you generally have to know someone powerful for that. He then asked if I knew anybody powerful; I told him I didn't; he said it was a pity.

Then he told me not to worry because executions are really quite humane now. The government spent a lot of time perfecting them, and the executioners are topnotch professionals who've really mastered their craft, not the drunken butchers sometimes employed in the past. Plus it wouldn't happen right away. Despite the new streamlined enforcement process, if I was lucky it might be a month before sentence was carried out, maybe longer, that one of his clients actually lasted more than a year, but that was probably a computer error. The last time we spoke, three weeks or so ago— it's hard to keep track of time when each day is exactly like the others—he told me my last appeal failed, that he'd look for some way to make another, but he had hundreds of other clients to deal with, too, all facing the same thing so, "Don't hold your breath." Those were his last words to me. I don't think it was a horrible joke at the expense of a man sentenced to die in one of the state's new, relatively painless gas chambers, just the words of the world's most jaded lawyer, which is to say any lawyer practicing now.

Despite the solitary confinement, there's something nice about the massive holding facility I've been in since my arrest—no executions are carried out here. It's a modern, austere, but clean place, and almost entirely automated. The days of cells with bars, doors that clang, and guards on catwalks with rifles are long gone. In fact, day to day you never see a guard, let alone another prisoner, and the cells themselves are more like small hotel rooms than the jail cells you see in popular media. Meals are delivered three times a day by a little robot that looks something like a cross between a free roaming nightstand and a trashcan on wheels, and other than being too fatty, too salty, and too sweet, I can't complain about the food, but I have a feeling the authorities want plump, logy prisoners. Clean bedding is brought and taken away weekly by the same robots. The high definition video screen is on sixteen hours a day, though you can't choose the content, and every other day you get a really nice private shower, though you never know when it will be. It seems to be entirely at the whim of whatever AI controls the place for reasons only it understands, but when it's time the bell rings and the cell door opens automatically. You follow a trail of little lights in the ceiling to your assigned shower vestibule. Sometimes many seem to be in use simultaneously, sometimes just a few. When you enter the door automatically closes behind you and you undress, deposit your dirty uniform down the laundry chute, then a door to the stall opens, closes behind you, and you get ten minutes of sauna hot water. As it's the only time you get out of your cell and the water is so soothing it's something you look forward to. When the shower ends you walk into the drying vestibule which seals behind you. Hot air comes up through the grated floor—it's a bit like standing inside a giant hot air hand dryer, and almost as soothing as the water. When it's done a bell rings and the door ahead opens. There's a clean uniform waiting and you put it on and walk back to your cell.

If you have no goals, no desires, and don't mind someone else making your every decision it's not a bad way of life. As a matter of fact, I think many people would welcome it, and the fact that maybe they thought I wouldn't is the reason I'm here. You may ask what happens if you don't honor their honor system—if you refuse to walk to the shower or back when the bell rings. That's happened twice since I arrived. That's when the guards come, lots of them, in helmets, carrying batons and shields, and they drag you away— and you know that because it's shown on the video screens live as they do it. What happens to those people isn't hard to guess because they're never shown being dragged back to their cells.

So when that beautiful warm water stops I go straight into the drying vestibule and a few minutes later, warm and dry, the air stops and I stand and wait for the little bell to ring and the door ahead of me to open. The bell rings as usual, but this time instead of the door in front opening, a door on the right swings open and I'm facing two large, scowling, steroid infused guards in a small room standing on either side of a clothes rack from which are suspended a number of strange harnesses made from wide black leather straps.

One yanks me forward, angrily orders me to stand legs apart on a black line painted on the white floor, hands behind my head, while the other snatches a harness from the rack, and together they begin wrapping me in it, pulling the straps so tight I swear it's like they're trying to crush my bones, but I don't dare utter a whisper of complaint for fear of what they'll do to me if they have the excuse; guys like this are always looking for an excuse. When they're done I'm bound in something reminiscent of the safety harnesses worn by high workers, only more so. Sturdy straps wrap around my waist, chest, and the top of each thigh. Vertical straps link them, some in front, some in back, a pair crisscross over my chest, and others run over each shoulder. Additional straps secure each wrist to the waist strap, and a final strap wraps around my elbows and tightens behind my back so they're pulled behind me, pinioning my arms. They're obviously experienced. I doubt it took them thirty seconds from start to finish.

Almost the instant they're done a young woman walks in and casually reaches for me with one outstretched hand. She's not in uniform. Her dress is incredibly informal—a baggy checked cotton shirt reaches almost all the way to the frayed hems of her faded denim cutoffs, and well worn brown hiking boots with down turned wool socks complete her ensemble. Her vegan skinny legs contrast with a butter fed round face that can barely contain the dazzling white teeth of an overly friendly smile verging on grin. Most notable about her, though, are her skin and hair. The former is bronzed, radiant, healthy. The latter is sun bleached, shines, and is pulled into a ponytail with the aid of an old rubber band. You get the feeling she hikes to the top of some remote ridge every Saturday just to feel the wind on her face when she clears its lee, and every Sunday plays beach volleyball in a skintight bikini with such abandon she doesn't notice that guys stare and fantasize as she sweats and jumps, and wouldn't care if she did.

Without a word of explanation she takes hold of my upper arm with a warm hand and leads me away like a pet at the animal shelter, out of the room and down a hall. As I want to get as far away from those goons as fast as I can I don't hesitate for an instant, just move in the direction her gentle pressure indicates. When we're out of earshot she says, "Don't worry, those guys are pretty intense, but they're OK, really."

I want to tell her she's mistaken, but I settle for asking, "What's happening? I didn't do anything."

"Don't worry, you're not being punished. It's just a prisoner transfer," she tells me. "Sorry about the harness. I know it's a bit restrictive, but it really does make this easier for everyone."

"Don't I get a uniform?"

"Nope, no way, not a chance. It might seem strange, and it was a little before my time, but out of spec prisoner uniforms caused, like, major headaches once. I can't go into details, but, trust me on this—it made so much work they just said, 'Never again,' and started

15

transferring prisoners *au naturel*."

"How could clothing cause problems?"

"You don't want to know," she replies with a chuckle. "Trust me, stuff of nightmares, but the poor bastards who wore them had to do something twice they didn't want to do once. If I could tell you, you'd say, 'No uniform, please,' to avoid any possibility of having it happen to you. Prisoners and staff would definitely be in like, total agreement on this one. Besides, nobody's going to see you except interested parties, no windows from here to there."

"Can you at least loosen the harness?" I ask. "They pulled it really tight."

"It's supposed to be tight," she tells me cheerfully.

"Please."

"You won't be in it forever—two, three hours max, then it'll be like it was never there."

I try to relax, concentrate on walking, feeling the smooth cool floor beneath my feet with every step, but the idea of being squeezed like this for hours pushes me towards panic. "I really think... there's something wrong," I tell her with forced calm.

The bronze lady brings me to a halt. She runs a finger under the strap running just beneath my armpits. "Take a nice deep breath for me," she says, her friendly manner now flavored with magnanimity, "...and another... It might seem too tight, but it's actually a really good fit, textbook stuff, and it's for your welfare. You could hurt yourself trying to get free, so it's important you can't, but it's also important for your psychological well-being to know you can't. Just because those guys are scary doesn't mean they don't know their stuff. They're actually pretty tiptop."

"It feels like I'm being crushed every time I take a breath."

"Well, we can't have that, but it would be unprofessional of me to second guess the guards' work, or more precisely, to act on your second guessing of their work, but maybe I can help. Press yourself flat against the wall," she advises, turning me to it. "Now exhale and suck in your tummy as far as you can." As soon as I do she jabs a knobby knee into the small of my back and cinches the strap around my lower torso even tighter, pulling it so taut that my pelvis seems to bulge when she's done. "Seems silly, but if you're feeling this one you won't feel the other, and the pressure down here will fade into the background because it's not associated with breathing."

"Thanks," I say, and though it feels like a boa constrictor has wrapped itself around my midsection it is, somehow, better.

"Just trying to help. Anything else?"

"This transfer—is it bad news?"

"There's no such thing as good or bad news," she tells me. "You do what you can in this world, right? And if you're lucky you can change things, but if you're unlucky you can still be the change."

"What I want to know is—is the place you're taking me a place where... sentences are carried out?" I ask, hating her new age newspeak, but using the broadest

17

language I can so I don't have to say the words.

"Oh, yes," she says. "That's why you're going."

"That means a date's been set?"

"Technically, the AI put you on the schedule seconds after you were convicted."

"When will it be?" I ask.

"Oh," she says sympathetically, "I can't tell you that. The countdown to the big day causes lots of anxiety, so we don't do it anymore; it's not right. Besides, schedules get moved around. It's all fluid now, designed for maximum efficiency. Some go at their scheduled time. Some go after, some before. It would be really cruel to tell somebody they've got three weeks then come for them in three days, especially if they ask why and you have to tell them, 'People arrested in that district need to be executed by the end of the fiscal year to ensure funding for the next,' or something like that."

"It can be three days?" I ask, the when rather than why being of more interest to me.

"I'm really not supposed to tell you this, but sometimes prisoners are executed within three days of arrest, not just conviction, and it can be even less. It doesn't happen often, but it happens. How long ago were you convicted?" she asks.

"I don't know, a month?"

"That's about right for the transfer order these days, so they didn't put a rush on you or anything. It looks like they're just sending you through at the normal rate, nothing special. That's something, right?"

'Nothing special,' the words echo through my

psyche, through my whole empty existence. I've never been anything special, and unless something extraordinary happens I never will be, nothing in life, forgotten in death. "That is something," I tell her. "But, after we get there—will it be soon?"

She pulls me gently away from the wall and turns me to face her, then takes a step back, forcing an empathetic smile to conceal her bleeding heart pity. "Sooner than you want, almost definitely," she says, her hair seemingly catching every ray of light and scattering it for fun, "but that's almost always the case, and it's a good thing when you think about it. It means you haven't given up, and that's such a positive. I mean, you see so many people walking down the street, dead eyed, hunch shouldered, and here you are, and you should have no hope, but your eyes are alive, and you'd stand tall if those straps would let you. It shows the indestructibility of the human spirit."

Everything about her look and demeanor says she's a practical and hands on young woman, which is in such contrast to her rainbow and puffy cloud philosophy, and the vicious hierarchy she serves. These things shouldn't co-exist in one personality. They can't cancel each other out. They should make her brain melt. I almost ask if she's ever seen an execution, ever seen a corpse, something to shock her into understanding that it's the destructibility of the human body that's my biggest concern, and should be hers, but I can't. I don't think I'm as worried about damaging her innocence as I am that she might answer, 'Yes,' and

19

damage mine. "It's just... I don't want to get closer," I finally say, hoping honesty will get through to her.

"We all get closer every minute," she replies with a sage smile, "sentence or not. I mean, I could drop dead right here, right now."

"But nobody's planning to kill you, and lots of people are planning to kill me—those guards... even you, at least indirectly."

"True, but I've got nothing against you, not personally. If it were up to me I probably wouldn't do it, but it's not. Those above us say you've got to go, so go you do, and it must really suck, but still, if I wasn't here somebody else would be, and they might not be as nice, might not maintain a positive outlook. See? I'm doing what I can. And where I'm taking you, it really is a nice facility, clean, and well organized, you'll see. It's lovely to work there. Plus, and you probably won't understand, but I feel like I'm accomplishing something, and I've got the best boss. She really knows her stuff. I learn something every day. And do you know the best part?" she asks.

"No."

"The faces, all the new interesting faces I get to see every time I come here for transfers. It's a real cross-section of society. I love that."

A second passes before it registers, and another before I can bring voice to the thought, "That means the people you took before..." I can't finish, though.

"Sadly, yes."

"And the next time they send you here..."

She gives a sympathetic smile and nod. "Neither of us can control that. If it helps think of this as like an escape room challenge. How are you going to get out of this trap?"

"I'm not going to get out of it. Nobody gets out of it."

"Of course you won't. I mean, everyone gets out eventually, just not the way they want, but you can still look for a secret tunnel to go through, or an access hole in the floor that leads to the sewers so you can dramatically dive in and swim out, right? You probably won't find them. This isn't a video game, and you don't get three lives, but where's the fun if you give up? And when it's over you'll be nothing so it won't matter if you feel silly looking for the improbable now."

"No, I guess it won't," I say darkly. "Will I see you after today?" I ask.

"No."

"Why not?"

"I can't go where you're going."

It doesn't surprise me that they don't want someone like her working on death row, even if she doesn't actually see the executions, but it means I have to ask now just in case she was hinting at something. She's the first person I've encountered since my arrest who doesn't seem to bear me actual animosity. I'm not foolish enough to think she likes me, but she's treating me like a ranch hand treats an animal—giving it feed and shelter and maybe even a friendly pat on the hindquarters now and then until it's time to send it to slaughter, and even then it's still a friendly hand to get it to move up the ramp and onto the truck. And every once in a while there's a story on the news of a cow that escaped from a slaughterhouse and ran down a highway trying to find freedom, and it always ends with a smiling bleached tooth reporter telling the viewers that the recaptured animal, which is somehow always apprehended in a burger joint's parking lot so it makes for great video, just couldn't wait to get on the menu, really funny stuff, but it's not cruel because by the time the story airs it's been hours since she was returned to the plant, and she's long since been reduced to hamburger, offal, hide, hooves and bones, like the less rebellious members of her herd who accepted their fate with less anxiety.

I take a few deep breaths looking into bright eyes that seem too innocent to understand the gravity of what she's a part of, what we're a part of, but if I'm going to ask it'll have to be now. "You seem to know a lot—the ins, the outs, and you're different from the others. Is there anything you can do for me?" I ask bluntly. My words are tinged with hopelessness, but I had to ask.

"I pretty much do the scheduling and the moving around and the general cleaning up. I can help with those. I will help with those. You can't stop me from helping with those, but that's not what you mean, is it?"

"No."

"You know, when it happens it won't make me happy, but I'll probably be satisfied, because it's our

22

job, and it's never personal. I thought you should know," she tells me.

"Are you sure there's nothing else you can do?"

"Sorry," she says, shaking her head. "Wait," she adds, brightly. "Yes, this might help." She slips something out of a small holster that had been concealed by her baggy shirt—a polymer handgrip with a button for her thumb and a pair of long needle-like electrodes at its end.

"Please don't," I say. "I'm not resisting. I saw a woman stunned once. It was horrible."

"I'm sorry."

"She died."

"Oh, that is regrettable," the bronze lady tells me with an exaggerated frown that somehow seems genuine.

"They would have killed her, anyway," I say, my eyes glued to the sharp, gleaming projections on the weapon.

"Then no harm done, but this isn't a stun gun—last thing I need is to have you twitching on the floor drooling for five minutes. It's an animal prod, same principle, lower voltage, but instead of immobilizing it encourages movement. One zap will get a nervous sheep into a sheering pen or the most stubborn little piggy onto a pork plant's kill line. Some prisoners don't want to go unless they can say they put up a fight. It makes them feel better, but they go just the same, and all I have to do is push a button," she says, slowly running the cold points of the electrodes against the soft

23

skin of my buttocks, lowering them until her hand pushes between my legs and they're against my scrotum. "Want one? It really will make you look eager to get where we're going."

A shiver runs down my spine and I shake my head nervously.

"Then move," she tells me happily, giving me a skin stretching push with the prod which I respond to instantly. She keeps its points against me as we continue our journey. I'm not sure if she wants to press the button or just bask in the ability to do it, but it doesn't make any difference when you're in my position, so I'm careful to match her pace. I don't want to know what it's like to be a sheep in her world, or a pig. "And most are like you," she adds as we walk, her body leaning against mine in a too familiar, possessive way that makes me as uncomfortable as the pointed electrodes, "content to just go when it's time, because it really is easier, but I enjoy it either way."

We round a bend in the hall. Immediately in front of us is a vehicle which has backed up to the building the way a truck backs up to a loading dock. It has a wide cargo door at the rear that opens to expose the passenger compartment, if that's what you call it. It's probably a modified bus, but with no windows in it or in the center's walls there's no way to be sure. What faces us is, essentially, a large, deep, nearly empty, windowless metal cube, with a solid front partition that separates it completely from the driver's compartment, more like a smooth walled shipping container than anything else. From the roof hang two parallel reinforced rail-like structures that run its entire length. From these are forty pulley-like attachment points, twenty on each side, each separated by about two feet. If I have any questions about how the harness system works they're answered with one glance at the single passenger already there. She is at the far left, suspended from her point facing us.

She's young, but an old young, with an ideals worn face, flyaway hair, and a freckled, skinny, long limbed, full breasted earth-mother's body, which is horribly exposed by the way the chest strap pushes those breasts slightly down, making them even more pendulous than they'd be if hanging naturally, and by the way most of her weight is borne by the two wide thigh straps which spread her legs indelicately. The blush that reddens her cheeks makes it obvious that she isn't expecting to see a man, but the days of gender segregation in prisons ended when those in power decided biological separation isn't cost effective and impedes progress. And despite an undeniable sexual attraction, it's not like I'd want to take advantage of her helplessness, and being just as restrained as she it really isn't an issue.

"Try not to worry about things you can't control," the bronze lady tells me as she walks me into the bus. "You'll know when it's time, and trust me, you'll handle it just fine. You all do. I'm so impressed by that. Before that try to appreciate every minute because none of us are guaranteed another. You just had a warm shower. You're nice and clean. The harness doesn't

25

pinch and nobody expects a thing from you. A lot of people would love to have such a trouble-free existence. The only difference between them and you is somebody told you, you're going to die, and you believe them, and nobody's told them, so they pretend they're going to live forever, and that lie eventually kills them, just like the truth will eventually kill you, and wouldn't you rather be killed by the truth than a lie?"

I can't stand this. I want to rebel. I want to stop. I don't want to end up like the earth-mother, suspended and helpless, but even if I was willing to accept the high voltage shock, and the inevitability of starting again, those electrodes really are sharp, and there's the possibility the bronze lady might inadvertently drive them through my skin if I hesitate, that each of my testicles might be impaled before she pushes the button and the current starts flowing, electrifying them from the inside, possibly destroying their sensitive tissue, or leaving them infected and pus filled before my 'big day' as she put it, and it wouldn't delay my trip to death row, not even for a minute, so I let myself be positioned under the pulley system directly in front of the suspended woman, let the bronze lady turn me so my back is to her and I'm also facing the rear of the bus. She frees a narrow folded strap at the top center back of my harness, threads it through the wheel mechanism and pulls. A heavy duty ratchet clicks ominously for a second or two as she raises me a few inches almost effortlessly, then twice more, hoisting me like a butcher

26

ready side of beef, until my feet, like the woman's, are almost a foot in the air. The weight is taken mostly by the thigh straps which spreads the load between the area just under my butt cheeks and my inner thighs, and though they pull my legs apart as indiscreetly as my earth-mother companion's, the straps are wide enough that it's not terribly uncomfortable.

The bronze lady seems to be reading my mind. "Most of the weight is transferred into that pretty pelvis of yours," she says, touching where it bulges beneath the harness' waist belt, "strongest bone in the body. Of course, it's not indestructible. I mean, every part of us is pretty transient when you think about it, but it'll keep you right here waiting for me until I take you down."

"When will that be?"

"When it's time."

"It feels strange," I say.

"It's a bit like floating, isn't it?" she asks, and strangely, she's right. I mean, the straps are still punishingly tight, and maybe that's why those supporting me don't seem so bad, and I'm still completely exposed, and feel horribly vulnerable with my elbows and wrists restrained—but somehow it is almost like floating.

I give her a hesitant half nod.

She glances at her fitness watch. "Look at that, you're done for the day and it isn't even lunchtime. All you have to do now is relax and let it all happen around you." She pulls a small hand-held scanner from her belt and runs it over my lower back where the prisoner chip is implanted. It beeps. "And that was your very last hand scan. It's all automated from here out, scans at every door—date, time, location, and biometrics recorded, from now until your chip's retired and they send me back for new transfers, your trip through the system as thoroughly documented as if you were a scented candle going cross country to a little old lady in Stockton. Now, play nice you two," she says, giving me a little push that sets me swinging as she walks away. In the near silence of the bus I can hear the leather creaking gently the first few times I reach the apex of my arc, and it's a soothing motion, soothing sound. The lady's made me into a pendulum, and pendulums don't have to worry about anything except someone forgetting to wind the clock.

When I've almost stopped moving she returns with a tightly harnessed and shopworn soccer mom type whose pre-arrest dye job has left her with rather lifeless two toned hair, dark to faded blonde. Her all over spray-on tan is also turning. The highest friction areas are blotchy white, the lowest a sad orange tinted brown, and everything in between is mottled and as dull as her hair. She stares straight ahead, and her breasts, fronted with unusually large and dark areolae and matching nipples, sag only slightly, and jiggle more than their modest size would suggest. There's something familiar about her, as if I'm looking at a high school sweetheart after ten years in a loveless marriage and dead end job, and that's when I realize—those ten years have taken less than two months. I wasn't sure until I saw her most striking feature, but those wide empty eyes are still an amazing shade of blue—she's the woman I was arrested with, very much alive, though a few pounds heavier and showing her age.

Either that jolt of electricity or her time alone has done its work. Her fight is entirely gone. She seems dazed, not even half there. I don't think she notices me or the other woman as the bronze lady guides her to the pulley ahead of me like a farm girl proudly leading her nervous pig into the judging ring at the county fair. As she reaches it she looks into my face and I see the flash of recognition. Her mouth opens. "Call my lawyer," she gasps, the words spoken like she's just awoken from a sound sleep, but she's already being rapidly spun about, hoisted off her feet, the harness cupping her ass cheeks and spreading her legs unceremoniously as it takes her weight. She struggles energetically for a few seconds until she realizes the futility of her efforts. "The straps," she complains, finding her voice, which is harsh and nasal, the kind that sounds the same whether counting jumping jacks while watching a fitness video or whispering, 'I love you,' meaninglessly in the dark after you've dismounted. "They're going to leave marks."

"They will," the bronze lady tells her calmly, running a finger along the fat bulging from around the thick leather bands encircling her thighs, "but they won't be bad."

"I don't..." she replies tensely, on the verge of panic. "I don't want marks."

"I can promise you," the bronze lady tells her softly,

putting her hands on the woman's hips gently, pressing her body to her back, sliding her hands down and in until they're cupping her inner thighs, "they'll be completely gone in less than three hours."

"You can promise?"

"I can promise. I do promise," she says.

"I don't want anybody to see them. If they have to see me naked I don't want them to see the marks."

"And nobody ever will."

"Really?" she asks.

"Really, now just relax, you don't have to push your tush back; you don't have to suck your tummy in. This is the only place in the world where it doesn't matter what you look like. There," she coos as the woman relaxes, "you're completely equal with everybody else. There's nothing shiny left to grab, no reason to flit here and there. You're only going to be judged once more, ever, and it'll be by how you react, not the evanescent package the fates wrapped your tiny birdlike soul in."

"I... I," the woman starts. She jumps at the sound of the beep as the scanner is waved over the small of her back.

"You leave everything to me now," the bronze lady advises. "If you get scared you just concentrate on the straps' snugness and pretend it's me hugging you. That goes for you two, too," she adds, looking to the earth-mother and me. "You're my beautiful bubbles floating on the summer breeze ephemeral, here iridescent with rainbow souls in my charge one moment, a few droplets of spent liquid plunging to the thirsty earth the next," she tells us, then leaves.

When she's clear I get a good look at the leotard woman's back, though she'll never be leotard woman to me again. Her left shoulder has a small red heart tattoo peeking out from under one of the black harness straps. Low on her right butt cheek is a four leave clover. But the cake taker is a large nauseating tramp stamp of elaborate curvilinear scroll-work surrounding the words, 'No Fear,' in careful script, inscribed in the trampiest place for a tramp stamp, as much upper ass as lower back, its southernmost scroll flourishes dipping well beneath crack top in places. I don't want to judge her, especially because she seems so unhappy with the flesh the fates have provided her with, but in the circumstance it's impossible not to. The harness presents her ready for inspection, and also prevents any attempt at modesty or egress. And maybe I shouldn't be harsh because I know the woman behind me is also judging what she sees, but I have eyes—and she's right in front of them, and I can't help that the artifacts of her desperate grab at fading youth make her particularly pathetic, but I'm sure I don't judge her as harshly as she judges herself when she looks in the mirror. Despite her smallish strange breasts and full thighs she probably hates, her narrow waist, wide hips, and rounded ass make her an attractive woman, at least sexually. Sometimes women allow themselves to believe they're not pretty because they're not young, or they don't look exactly like some digitally manipulated photograph, but the truth is relatively few sex identifiers—wide hips,

31

full breasts, relatively hairless skin—are all any woman needs to send the message that she's a potential mate.

If there'd never been any reforms, and the stars had aligned, I would have taken her home the day we were grabbed, because when she ran by I got a glimpse of her full little hands pinioned at the small of her back when maybe my eyes were drawn to something a bit lower, and there wasn't a ring on any of her fingers, and women of that age without rings are taking no chances. They're making sure everyone knows they're available, so there's a middling chance that when I walked back with my milk she would have been at one of the little bistro tables in front of the juice bar wearing blackout sunglasses to hide the fine crows' feet that were getting a little deeper every year, a pale floral ankle length slit skirt, and thick soled designer flip-flops, telling herself she was just sitting at the table closest to the sidewalk for her post yoga health drink, something like a milkshake thick carrageenan infused pulpy guava juice with colloidal mineral shot and heavy cream float, no cinnamon, because she wouldn't have wanted to admit to herself it was really so every guy who walked by could get a look at her nipples under the taut paper thin fabric of her mostly dry leotard, and they'd all see through her as easily as they saw through it, and so would I, but I'd have stopped and smiled and talked to her, allowed myself to get lost in those luminous blue eyes, and if she'd unartfully crossed her legs so the slit opened and exposed them from ankle to thigh I'd have known she'd not only give me a ride home, but a ride

32

between them when we got there. Oh, she'd complain she was a mess, that she'd just worked out, as if stretching in a hot room is a workout, and that she needed a shower, but we would have been in her car in ten minutes, in my bed in twenty.

I would have regretted it before we got there. I would have really regretted it after I saw those tattoos, all of which would have been concealed by that leotard until I slid it off her shoulders and down to her ankles gently, but with enough force to signal her not to resist, but I wouldn't have regretted the five minutes I was inside her, or how desperately she clung to me, or even her little mousy squeaks as I gave it to her hard while approaching climax. But after? After I would have made some excuse to get her out quick. If she'd headed for the bathroom I'd have told her the hot water heater was broken. I've had ladies like her draw piping hot baths and luxuriate in long soaks while I cooled my heels locked outside, unable to wash their smell and drying fluids off of me, and I don't think I should have to wash my dick in the sink at my own place. Then one, when she finally sauntered out of my bathroom prune-like and blotchy pink, declared herself a ghost because she knew she'd melted and gone down the drain with the bathwater, but when I proved she was still all too corporeal by poking her hot back fat with a cold finger it didn't leave her best pleased, but she did leave. Luckily, I've yet to entertain a woman like her who didn't just reach for her clothes when I said, "But if you don't mind a cold shower..."

And I think I would have been downright revolted as I watched No Fear bend over to stuff her soft little body back into that skin thin leotard no matter how perfect its beige paint job or how much body oil she'd slathered on herself that morning, but I would have smiled approvingly if she looked up at me uncertainly as she did. I would have dutifully plugged her number into my phone as we said our goodbyes and only blocked it after she drove away, but she wasn't naive— narcissistic, maybe, but not naive. She would have known the odds of that encounter turning into forever were a thousand to one before she stepped out of the polyester I'd pooled at her feet to get into my bed, but maybe what she needed that day wasn't being tackled on concrete and a hundred thousand volts electrifying her rib cage, but a few minutes of passion on a stranger's mattress and a trip home in sweat smelling fabric with a slow spreading wet spot at the crotch because we can't all be lifelong loves, can we? We get to grab some freedom, too, right? And nothing says freedom like ghosting a clingy lover with an aging body and a high opinion of herself, because I can't imagine anything worse than being doomed to be with her forever, spend the rest of my life exhausting my passion against her soft little tattooed body, even if it does have the right shape.

Does that make me a bad person? Yeah, probably. And does her demanding self-centered self-delusion make her a bad person? Yeah, probably. But bad enough to be here? Bad enough to be transferred to a place where lives end, with a countdown timer we can't see running, never knowing which day they'll drag us off and fill our lungs with poison? Besides, maybe loosing yourself in passion for a few minutes, connecting with another person through these imperfect bodies until the warm viscid demands of biology are met, is enough to change the world because none of us are the result of the eternal bonding of two shining immortal souls called into existence by perfect philosophies. We're here because of a somewhat messy minutes long bonding of flesh that's all too fragile, and transient.

The bronze lady returns about once a minute with another harnessed prisoner whose flawed and transient flesh's destiny has also been adjudicated, and found lacking, always alternating between women and men, suspending each from a pulley, then checking their chips, until all forty attachment points have someone suspended beneath them. Nothing seems to link us but a certain averageness and having been condemned and assigned to this bus at this time. The only prisoner of note is an obviously pregnant woman who's suspended from a point on the other side of the bus near its back. The strap cutting into her bulging belly looks especially cruel, and though she isn't in obvious distress I'd think they would have given her a break and let her stay where she was for a couple of months so she wouldn't have to endure being handled like this in her condition. It's not like they need her near a gas chamber now, anyway, but I'm afraid that's an old fashioned way of thinking. For all I know they're planning on forcing a cesarean birth and dragging her away for execution a day later. I hope when the reformers say that no one is above the law, and no one can delay the law, they haven't abandoned the last of their humanity, but it's difficult to speak in absolutist terms without sounding like you're willing to do anything. What the baby's more deserving adoptive parents will tell the child when she's old enough sets my teeth on edge. I hope they have the good grace to leave it at, 'She died,' but they probably have to agree with the reforms so fervently that they may delight in saying more, and I shudder to think what will happen to that child if she doesn't ardently espouse the reforms that are about to cost her, her mother.

I'd be lying if I said being in this windowless box as it filled didn't give me a slightly uneasy feeling, and I suppose I wouldn't really want there to be windows so upstanding fathers driving their children to outings could point to us as examples of what happens if naughtiness carries through to adulthood, but seeing every attachment point used does make me feel more at ease. Though I normally despise herd mentality there's no way around the simple fact—the more people they have to kill the more likely I am to survive a little longer. It's strange to think that my hope lies in the deaths of those around me, but their hope lies in mine, giving us a kind of brutal equality, playing a zero sum game we're all predestined to lose. At around a month since conviction my time should be running out, but maybe it won't be tomorrow, or even this week. Maybe being nobody special, always pushed to the back, always ignored, always invisible, will save me, the cape-less comic book hero who, like every other, had a superpower all along but didn't realize it until it was time to save the world, or the little piece of it I call my life. When we arrive at the new prison I just need to figure out a way to be more invisible than I've ever been, and if I'm lucky I'll get lost in the clutter of an AI's fuzzy logic, my mundane number always sorted toward the end of an ever changing list designed for efficiency and not order until some human notices or my luck changes and mine ends up at the front and they come for me, but if I last long enough to set a record my lawyer might remember me the way he couldn't remember my trial and hold me up as a shining beacon of hope for the hopeless, though that will be cold comfort when they're strapping me into the chair.

The No Fear lady's presence is frightening, though. She was arrested seconds before me, and here she is directly in front of me on the bus, both of us on our way to the place we're scheduled to die, which suggests that vaunted AI may sort us by time of arrest only. For all I know she was in the cell next to me all this time, had her trial exactly half an hour before mine, was advised by the same insensitive idiot not to hold her breath. Maybe she goes then I go, our order fixed—her, then me, then the earth-mother. If that's the case there are at least seventeen ahead of us, but it won't take them a year to kill eighteen people—nineteen. Maybe there's

37

no way to vanish. How did my lawyer's other client last a year? More importantly, how do I manage it?

Eighteen days or three hundred and sixty-five? Either way I guess there's a chance, a small chance, that things will change before they get to me, but in my brief study of history I've noticed that the pendulum tends to swing towards extremes faster than it swings away from them so I decide—I won't hold my breath.

When the last prisoner is hoisted off his feet the bronze lady picks up a small box near the back of the bus and begins doing something to each prisoner on my side. When she gets to me I see the box holds a bunch of plastic disks with metal tabs on the back that look a bit like electronic dog trackers. She lifts one and snaps it into place in a socket where two straps intersect at the center of my chest over my sternum.

"What's that?" I ask automatically. I'm the only one who has.

"Heart rate monitor—lets us know if you're in distress," the bronze lady replies, smiling warmly. Then she snaps one into place on the woman behind me, returns to the back, and though the box she had didn't seem anywhere near empty she puts it down, picks up another, and snaps what appear to be identical disks in the harnesses of the prisoners suspended from the rail on the other side. When she's done she picks up a tablet computer, taps out a brief message, then closes the door with her inside. The bus is in motion a couple of minutes later. She stands with the tablet at her side and leans against the door looking forward, and she smiles,

smiles all the time, smiles without making eye contact with any of us, just staring between the two rows of prisoners she's suspended as we gently move with the vehicle's motion. I'd say she's smiling like a fool, but she seems genuinely happy, and how is she the fool if we're the ones she's immobilized like this?

"How long will this be?" a man from somewhere ahead of me asks.

"Not long at all," she assures us.

They're the only words spoken during the journey, and true to her word it ends in just about as much time as it took to load the bus. It slows and makes a series of low speed sharp turns, going forward and backward a couple of times before finally coming to a halt.

"You see, not long at all," the bronze lady tells us, opening the door and stepping out. It's hard to see around all my fellow prisoners, but the large room beyond looks very much like the detention center we departed, clean and modern. A woman with sparkling eyes and pale white skin joins the bronze lady at the back of the bus. She's wearing an elegant black cocktail dress, its skirt cut below the knee, and toe baring low heels revealing a fresh pedicure and glistening black nail polish. She looks and moves like a guest at a dignified soiree, not someone who works at a prison, especially one where executions are carried out.

"Ready to offload," the bronze lady tells her.

"Good... good," the pale lady replies, cocking her head, looking into the bus curiously, scrutinizing every face before saying, "Unload group two."

The bronze lady taps at her tablet.

I'm shocked when everyone on my side of the bus begins moving towards the open door simultaneously. The rails that I'd assumed were just there for reinforcement, to spread the load of the harnesses, are part of some kind of conveyor system, probably concealing a chain drive something like a long garage door track. It hums gently and one by one we're transferred from the vehicle's rail to one suspended from the ceiling of the building. When it's my turn there's just the smallest bump as the transfer is made, and then I flow smoothly with the others until we're all well clear of the bus and the system stops, leaving us swaying gently in our harnesses.

We're in a largely empty 'L' shaped room that branches off to the right. The floor is white composite and highly polished. The walls are white and modern. The only thing really in the room are the two parallel conveyors suspended from the ceiling that vanish to the right as they turn to follow the room's shape.

"And group one," the pale lady instructs, and soon the group that was next to us in the bus is again by our sides.

Behind us I hear the bus door close, then the building's door is closed and locked, and the bus drives away.

"Where are we?" a man near the front in the other row demands. "Are you the warden? I want to see the warden. You can't keep us bound like this."

"There is no warden. This isn't a prison," the pale

lady tells us calmly. Her voice is somehow cool and warm at the same time. "It's a processing and disposal facility. Since the reforms we stopped telling prisoners their execution date. The countdown to the final day causes anxiety for them and their families," she tells us, echoing what the bronze lady told me. Then, after a brief pause, she adds, "Unfortunately, your time is up. In a few days your families will get letters informing them it happened today. It will be comparatively humane, and relatively fast, a few minutes of discomfort not much worse than trying to catch your breath after running as fast as you can for as long as you can. Try to relax. You're in good hands. We're professionals. We do this every day. You have nothing to worry about, ever again."

"What about my baby?" the pregnant woman blurts out.

The pale lady stops, looks at her and smiles as if she's just seen an old friend. "My goodness... you're big as a house," she tells her. "Don't worry. We'll have baby out of you in no time. We've got a special warm hydro bath where baby can swim right out of mommy." She raises her hands like she's going to gently stroke the woman's belly, but stops when they're mere inches away, then slowly withdraws them.

"Please, please," the woman immediately ahead of me says, her voice quavering, yet demanding. "My lawyer said he'd try to find a way to make an appeal."

The pale lady takes a dozen slow steps towards us, her narrow heels clicking languidly against the spotless floor. "I'm so glad to hear that," she tells her, "and if it comes through we'll pull you out of line and send you back. If it doesn't you'll be processed with the others."

"The bus is gone," she whispers desperately. "How can you send me back? The bus is gone. It's gone."

"Stay calm, no matter what happens we take care of everything."

I think I was in shock until that moment, and that's when I realize—the pale lady is going to kill her. She's going to kill the pregnant woman, and there won't be any water birth before she does. She's going to kill the rest of them. She's going to kill me. No matter what she says she's going to kill us. She will personally activate the death machine with her delicate hands with their perfectly manicured shining black nails. It might take her all day, but one by one she's going to take us down from these rails, guide us to a gas chamber, and kill us —no, not kill, process, and I know euphemisms are supposed to be horrible, invented and used by people doing something they know is wrong to disguise the reality of their actions, make the unthinkable palatable —execute means kill, process means execute, but I don't want to be killed; I don't want to be executed. If something's going to happen I'd prefer to be processed; I want that word used, especially if it's going to be done by a strangely calm, strangely attractive woman wearing a party dress and open toed heels whom you know never has trouble getting to sleep at night despite what she does all day. I can deal with the word 'process,' not the others. The result will be exactly the

42

same, but it sounds clean, inoffensive, and that's all I've got left.

The bronze lady approaches our executioner. "I think we're ready to begin," she says, handing her the small tablet computer.

White hands glide over it, make a few swipes and taps. "Not quite, one of the heart rate monitors is intermittent. It's in group two," she says pointing to the row I'm in. They begin walking, the pale lady between our two rows staring at the screen, the bronze lady on the outside. "Near the back... There, that one, she says," pointing to me.

"He won't be a holdout, one of the first to go, if you ask me."

"We owe it to them to be sure. It's probably just the contacts. Try some electrode gel."

The bronze lady reaches into the deep pocket of her oversized shirt and pulls out a small white tube similar to a travel sized toothpaste. She uncaps it and squeezes some clear jellylike substance onto a couple of her fingertips. "Just being honest," she tells me softly, almost apologetically as she pushes her fingers under the crisscrossed straps holding my monitor and rubs the cool substance back and forth almost sensually on the skin over my heart.

After a few strokes the pale lady's tablet beeps. "There, steady as an old clock," she says, holding the tablet for the other to see. I try not to look, but can't help it, and as I do I see twenty EKG-like graphs being continuously updated. I quickly avert my eyes, locking them straight ahead, but she's seen.

"It's OK. You can look," the pale lady tells me as calm and content as a woman picking flowers on a lazy spring afternoon, angling the screen so I can get a better look, and that's when I notice her lips aren't harsh like her nails. They're plump, and coated with a glossy medium pink lipstick that gives her face an almost angelic quality. "See, this is that row," she says, pointing to the prisoners suspended from the other rail and scrolling the screen, showing another twenty graphs. Then she scrolls back to the first screen and points to one of the graphs near the center, "and that's you. They're not in order. You're near the back. This is in the middle. They don't need to be in order for our work. We just have to know your group from theirs. There was an error message a minute ago. Now your signal's good. The squiggles are your heartbeats. They're normal, but a little fast, which is understandable. You're probably feeling some anxiety, but panic won't change your fate, nor will anything you do or say, so you really can just relax and experience it before it all goes away. When your line's flat processing is over, when the others are, processing for your whole group is complete. When theirs are flat," she says, swiping the screen and indicating the other row, "theirs is." She lowers the tablet and hands it to her assistant. I look straight ahead, but can see her, almost feel her, staring at me almost benevolently in my peripheral vision.

"You said it's like running," I say softly, trying to

ignore the beads of perspiration forming slowly on my brow. I don't know why I spoke. Everything she says is chilling no matter how calm and melodious her voice, no matter how mundane her euphemisms, and, barring a miracle, by the end of the day it won't matter, nothing will.

"Yes," she tells me brightly, "exactly. You see, the gas we use is called carbon dioxide. The technology was developed to slaughter pigs. Isn't that amazing? If we didn't have a taste for bacon we might not even be here, and it was easy to adapt. When you think about it most of our equipment was developed for dealing with delicious or unwanted animals. And carbon dioxide is perfect for the job, and much more humane and easier to work with than cyanide in its gaseous form, which is what they used to use. Cyanide is quick and effective, astonishingly so, and the effect was completely irreversible—one or two breaths of it and nothing will save you, which would make my job easier, but it's also intensely painful, which you wouldn't want, and there are safety concerns for the crews who have to work near it, but CO_2, that's another name for carbon dioxide, is perfect for the job. It's colorless, odorless, tasteless. It's one hundred percent effective, acceptably fast acting, acceptably humane. Technically, it isn't even a poison. It's an asphyxiant, and it's natural, biological. Without it there wouldn't be life. Your body makes it. It's what you expel when you breathe. It's what makes you want to take a breath when you hold it, not a lack of oxygen, but a buildup of carbon dioxide.

45

So, during initial processing I'll boost the levels quickly, but only to a certain point. One moment everything will be fine, just like it is now. A few breaths later you'll feel like you just ran harder than you ever have in your life, only you won't be able to catch your breath. You'll just keep breathing faster and faster and your heart will race like you never thought it could, but all you have to do is pretend you're a runner in the big championship race and you're going to win... And that's what we want, both of us. We want your heart pounding. We want you completely breathless. That's when I nudge the gas levels up, and your respiration will be so high that you'll pass out quite quickly, just slump over, out like a light. And that's it. It's over for you. That doesn't sound too bad, does it?"

I swallow. I give my head an almost imperceptible shake.

"You see? It's a win-win, but I still have work to do. If I just took you out of the chamber you'd wake up with nothing worse than a headache. Then you'd have to go through it all again. It's not horrible, but you don't want to have to do it twice, right? So I'll raise the gas levels high enough to induce cardiac arrest. That means your heart will stop. It's just a few percent higher, but I raise it relatively slowly to make sure you're in a deep sleep and stay there, because it would be painful if you were awake, but you're not, so you don't feel your heart spasm. You don't feel it stop. The last thing is to make sure it doesn't restart. That almost never happens, but I make sure. I raise the CO_2 level to one hundred percent, and if your heart should restart, if your lungs should spontaneously take a breath, that will stop them instantly so there's no chance you might jerk awake in pain, might feel yourself die. After a few minutes the cardiac arrest becomes irreversible, the brain dies, and that's when processing ends for me. And I don't want you to worry. I've done this many times before, many. Nobody wakes up."

"Thanks," I say, this time the whisper is so soft I barely hear it myself.

She gets even closer. "You don't need to thank me. I love my work... and I hope that didn't sound macabre, and I hope this doesn't sound macabre, either, but I see you as my customer, I really do. So I want to make this as easy as I can for you." Then, after a brief pause she asks, "Is there anything else?"

I nod.

"Ask."

I shouldn't—I can't stop her from killing me, and it shouldn't make any difference after you're dead, but it does, and I really don't want to know the answer, one answer, anyway, and those around me will hear it too, which might make it worse for them, but somehow I can't keep from speaking, "I heard a rumor that when the processing is over... you dissolve us in acid."

The pale lady's eyes open wide and she looks at me as if I've just blasphemed. "In acid?" she asks, but her voice doesn't rise. It remains calm and cool. "No, nothing could be further from the truth."

"It's just... what I heard."

47

"Shame on whoever told you that. It would be horrible, going where you're going, thinking that. People shouldn't spread rumors."

"Cremation then?" I ask. Destroying bodies in any way seems a kind of desecration, shows a contempt for our common humanity, but cremation wouldn't be that bad compared to acid—turned to gas, symbolically rising to the heavens beats being turned to sewage and piped away.

She shakes her head.

"Burial?" Somehow I imagined that dehumanization through death wouldn't be enough for the reformers, that they wouldn't be satisfied merely destroying lives, that they'd have to erase all evidence of our bodily existence to satiate whatever drives them.

The pale lady cocks her head curiously, lips parted. "Does it really matter?" she asks.

"No," I whisper. She's right. I'm sure there won't be any flowers, any words of remembrance, any gravestones, but an unmarked mass grave dug, filled, and compacted by a noisy yellow machine in some lonely place abandoned to nature isn't such a bad way to spend eternity. And maybe someday when the insanity ends, no, doesn't end, when it rests, or moves restlessly over the horizon, someone will innocently unearth a bone and ask who we were, maybe even who I was, and if they can't learn, as seems our fate, at least maybe they can remember.

"There's something else, isn't there?" the pale lady asks, dropping her voice even lower, her hazel eyes burning into me.

I nod, barely moving my head, teeth clenched, throat dry. I want to ask if I can go first. I don't want to see the people ahead of me taken away one by one, imagine them strapped to a chair in a gas chamber panting and gasping then going limp as she watches sedately through a window a few feet away. I certainly don't want that to be me, but the question is when, not if, and I'm not sure if I can take watching person after person led away and know what's happening to them, then having her come for me with her sparkling eyes. "Can I..." I start.

"Yes?" she replies instantly, curiously, inching towards me.

I don't have the courage. I'm afraid that no matter when I'm taken I'll be led away gibbering, that my legs will collapse, that they'll have to drag me to the chamber. I've lived a forgettable life. I don't want to be remembered for being unable to find a minute's courage, not after requesting it. I have to say something. Her eyes are boring into the side of my head. "Can I thank you again?"

She reaches up and lays a soft warm hand on my shoulder that sends a chill down my spine. "Of course," she tells me, "and you're very, very welcome," and with that she withdraws her hand, letting her fingertips linger on my skin for a few moments, then walks away between our two rows towards their front, giving me a good look at her pale calves and ankles.

"Advance group two, load position," she orders the

bronze lady, her voice like an autumn pond.

The latter swipes her finger across her tablet a few times in reply, and the twenty of us begin gliding smoothly forward under the rail, and it's like she said, like we're floating, floating just faster than the pale lady walks, and as I approach her I can't help looking at her hips rocking unhurriedly, at her bare skin that looks impossibly smooth, impossibly clean, impossibly white. Everything about her proclaims she isn't a taker of life, but this isn't a dream. In dreams you're just as helpless. You float along in them with the same tranquility, but they're not tethered to time. They're edited, like movies, but time is horribly, horribly linear in this nightmare world, the seconds ticking off silently one by one as if they're physically attached to a chronometer's beat.

I resist the urge to turn my head as I pass her, to look at the silhouette of her breasts beneath the black fabric, to see her moonlight face again. As we approach the turn in the overhead rails where they follow the room's shape to the right I see that ours continues straight a bit further than the one on our left, so that they'll still be parallel after the turn, but much closer together. It only takes a moment to round the bend and that's when I see them, two narrow shining brushed metal caverns that the rails run straight into. They share a common wall between them, and have matching solid vault-like doors, one that closes from the right, one from the left, each of which is open wide to allow unhindered access to the chambers they'll seal. They're narrow, just wide

50

enough for our shoulders, just high enough for the rails that carry our harnesses, and they're deep, at least ten, maybe twelve feet. Bright diffuse light from their ceilings makes the spotless brushed steel walls and floors gleam softly. The non-shared outside linear walls have full length grates a few inches high near both the top and bottom that look capable of changing the atmosphere inside in seconds.

We come to a stop.

The prisoner at the front is just a few feet from the mouth of the right chamber, which has the numeral '2' engraved in the otherwise unadorned metalwork near its top. It's the most terrifying thing I've ever seen, and not just because I know I'm scheduled to die inside it, and have been for weeks, since seconds after my conviction, but because it seems so perfectly designed for its purpose, because I know that yesterday, and the day before, and the day before that people were processed there, and when another group of prisoners hang in their harnesses staring into its depths tomorrow there won't be a trace I'd ever been there.

I'd been expecting what you see in the movies—a little room with a chair for the prisoner being killed and big windows for the executioner and witnesses to observe their struggles, the former with feigned gravitas poorly concealing repressed joy, the latter with ever increasing revulsion. But this is so much scarier, designed for efficiency, for speed. With the conveyor extending into it we won't even leave our harnesses. Our feet will never touch the ground again, at least until we're buried. Spaced every two feet or so each group occupies around forty linear feet, which means four or five of us will fit in each chamber at a time. If it takes ten minutes per batch I could be dead forty minutes after the pale lady starts, and she'll be working from a control panel a few feet to the right of the chambers.

It looks like the kind of thing you see white jacketed scientists sitting in front of in old movies documenting moon shots, with a myriad of controls and screens, one of which clearly shows our heart rates, a duplicate of what the pale lady showed me on the tablet. The others display graphs and numbers I don't understand, and don't want to, because I never want to use something like that, because nobody should. Beneath are buttons, switches, knobs and sliders. An ergonomic chair on casters that looks like it was designed for an architect, not a killer, is positioned in front of it. Is the pale lady really going to sit there and watch our hearts stop on the monitors with her lumbar supported? I mean, even if we've thought the wrong thoughts, even if some of us have done the wrong deeds, maybe truly horrible deeds, is this the best response a civilization can come up with? Technology advances, instincts don't, and that should terrify everyone, not just those waiting to die.

Behind us the order is given for group one to be advanced, and the rail next to us begins to hum. Soon the others slide around the bend. As its leaders pass they're so close I can feel the breeze each one creates as they go by, and when we're again next to each other their conveyor comes to a stop leaving each of them rocking in their harness gently. The pale lady walks to the chambers unhurriedly and looks into the mouth of each one, examining them slowly though they're both empty and utterly spotless. Not even a single fingerprint mars their gleaming surfaces. Even if she's being paid to kill us she must be thinking what I'm thinking looking into those empty spaces just tall and wide enough for us—no matter how clean and shiny they are, no matter how bright, no human being could willingly put another inside something like that to die. She looks to her assistant.

"Disposal doors closed and locked, one and two," the bronze lady gives in reply to a question that seems to have been asked telepathically, and she knew she was bringing me to this when she walked me to the bus so helpfully, so cheerfully. She knew I'd never take another step when she hoisted me off my feet, knew I'd be in that shining metal box minutes after arriving, knew I'd die in it when she smiled and said, 'You're done for the day and it isn't even lunchtime,' even made me grateful she tightened the harness that made me so easy to control. This was all waiting, all ready. None of it was an abstraction for her. And after? Will she eat a sandwich and an apple while our glassy eyed bodies are stacked somewhere under a tarp, cooling, and drink masala chai tomorrow on her break when we're being compacted under a yard of freshly moved earth by a bulldozer in the middle of some barren alkali flat marked only by a rising cloud of white dust that's just a smudge on the horizon from the nearest road? But at least they'll take these crushing harnesses off before that happens. The bronze lady promised they'd come off, that we'd be naked when we were returned to the earth, like when we were born. It shouldn't matter. Nothing should matter, but burying the dead still bound would be an act of utter contempt, and I wouldn't want to molder with the skin of the unfortunate cow that became its straps.

Satisfied that the chambers are ready the pale lady nods to the bronze, then saunters to the control desk and sits, running a finger down what must be the most important indicators and switches before pivoting in her chair so she can look at us. Is she really going to leave us hanging here as she works, getting a good look at what she does, as we move five spaces closer to the front with every batch? At least without windows we won't have to watch the others die, but what about those inside, only able to see those ahead of them and steel walls inches away?

"Load chamber two," the pale lady says, her voice still even, still tranquil. There's a momentary disconnect, or an instant's disbelief. I heard the words, but... Her assistant is already tapping the tablet. Almost instantly all twenty of us begin sliding forward. This is it, the start. The first five of us are going in right now. I'm terrified just getting closer to that life ending chasm, so scared I'm dizzy. If I'd volunteered to be first I'd be on my way into it right now, fully aware I'd never leave, that only the empty shell that used to contain whatever it is that's me would be left when it

54

was over, that somehow I'd vanish in there, be drained away forever in just a few minutes by something I can't see, can't smell, can't taste. Forty minutes of extra life seems like an eternity now, forty minutes without a single complaint about being immobilized, suspended, the raw material at the input end of a modern factory that produces corpses. Can this really be run by only two people, one too innocent and one too sophisticated to be here? One happy to be doing it, the other benignly undisturbed?

"Why us?" a woman near the front snaps, voice rising, pivoting her head towards our executioner. We're in front of a chamber marked number two. Surely number one should be first. We must all be thinking it. We must all want to know. Almost the instant she speaks her head pivots back, her fear palpable as she crosses the threshold of the gas chamber she'll be killed in.

It's hard to see with everyone ahead of me, but the chamber should be full. We've moved ten feet, about its depth, yet the conveyor doesn't stop, and prisoner after prisoner ahead of me glides into it. It's like those at the front have just vanished, like we're the material for a magician's grand finale. More disturbing, though, are ominous reverberant metallic clicks that begin emanating loudly from within every couple of seconds. With half our group in a chamber that should only hold a quarter of us I can see that there's still, somehow, space for more of us, many more—and then like a horrible lightning bolt out of a clear blue sky I understand how it works.

The overhead conveyors our harnesses hang from aren't permanently attached to the hidden chain in the rail that moves them. There's some kind of pawl mechanism that allows slippage, but only in one direction. It's as ingenious as it is terrifying. We can move forward, but not back, and if stopped those behind will just keep moving forward until they, too, are stopped. As the first prisoner reached the back of the chamber and hit the disposal door it didn't jam the drive. The conveyor simply released the chain and activated a locking mechanism to make sure he couldn't draw back even a millimeter. Then the next prisoner slid forward until she ran into him, and the next into her, the machinery neatly packing us into the chamber like sardines. The twenty of us are one mouthful for this thing. I've been helpless for weeks, but this is what it's like to feel truly helpless. I'm weak, nauseous. For a few seconds I think I may pass out.

As she approaches the chamber's opening the woman with the No Fear tattoo begins pivoting her head, looking from the bronze lady to the pale lady and back. "I want a blindfold. Don't I get a blindfold? Please?" she babbles, silencing herself the instant she crosses into it, and while any delay now would be welcome I'm glad they don't stop our ingress, that they haven't just forgotten them, though I get the feeling that neither lady forgets things when it comes to this. I certainly wouldn't want to feel either one of their soft bodies pressing against me as they reached up to take my sight. I'm sure the tattooed woman only asked because she thought it was something she was supposed to have, like perfectly tan skin, like blonde hair, like tribal ink showing allegiance to a clan that only ever existed in an advertising agency's media buys. But blindfolds, like the other elements of traditional execution, are outdated, quaint artifacts of a bygone time. Ostensibly they spared the condemned the stress of seeing themselves undergoing final preparations for their death machine, and of its activation, but I have a feeling they were more to spare the executioner from having to look into the terrified eyes of helpless people as they killed them, and their lifeless eyes after. Either way, I'm glad they engineered the new system like this. Nothing moves, and we'll never see colorless gas, so maybe there has been progress, if on the wrong front. I know I don't get to choose, but I wouldn't want to have my sight taken from me in my last moments. Humans are visual animals, and darkness is frightening when you're vulnerable, and I won't pretend I'm brave. If nothing else let it be warm, shiny and bright before everything goes away forever.

There's a little bump as I come to a transition in the rail, then another when I, too, cross the threshold, and my breath catches as the chamber walls fill my peripheral vision. No Fear comes to a sudden jiggling stop when she runs into the man ahead of her, her conveyor locking loudly as it does. A moment later, her flesh still undulating, I run into her, the impact harder than I'd imagined against such soft flesh. It's not enough to knock the wind out of me, but it's still jarring, makes everything too real as the conveyor above me locks in place with a reverberant rifle bolt click that keeps me molded to the warm smooth skin of her mottled torso, my body notched neatly between the points of her pinioned elbows, my fingertips touching the top of her wide pelvis. A moment later the earth-mother strikes me from behind just as hard, nesting against me the same way, her soft breasts flattening against my back as her conveyor locks.

The order is given to load chamber one, which happens without a word of dissent. Not even the pregnant woman protests, but I guess they saw what good it did us.

"Seal chamber two," the pale lady orders, her voice distorted by the acoustics of the narrow space.

The sound of the hydraulic actuator is louder than I expect and I jump, but I guess it has to be powerful as the door is about an inch thick, and appears to be solid steel. Its faceted edges are designed to mesh with the edges of the chamber to form a perfect gas tight seal. I pivot my head and watch it begin to close slowly. As it does a short section of rail leading into the chamber rises and pivots to give it clearance. All of us eventually learned our sentence, usually days after it was passed, 'Death by the inhalation of lethal gas at the earliest time practicable at a place chosen by the designated authorities and by method of their devising,' and chilling as those words were, and as horrible as it was to be judged unworthy even of existence, this machine, shining and functional, is their manifestation. I can't bring myself to watch the world outside vanish forever and turn my head forward to see the heads and straps the harnesses hang from ahead of me.

The hips of the woman behind me push forward slowly as the door closes against her buttocks, making her fit into this box, making us fit, pressing us together, the soft flesh of our bodies forced to conform to each other as it does, leaving us as close together as any lovers have ever been. A moment later the sharp metallic sound of the door's locking mechanism makes us all start. We're sealed in. It's instantly claustrophobic, and so surreal it isn't even dreamlike. It's going to happen. All of this was created so it would, but there's still this hollow disconnect ringing through my consciousness, the inability to believe this might actually be the end despite the evidence of my eyes and ears.

The sound of chamber one's door closing and locking are soft, but unmistakable as the preparations continue, step by methodical step.

The pale lady's soothing voice fills the chamber through an unseen PA system. "We're going to begin now. The first thing you'll hear are the recirculating fans start. Those are just to keep the atmosphere moving and blended—we want everyone getting a nice even mix. Shortly after you'll hear the gas injectors. As soon as you do just relax for me and take nice deep breaths and let it do its job. It'll be over before you know it."

59

And the lady near the front was right. It's not fair that we're going first, and even less fair that we don't know why we have to, and will never know. We're group two. We're in chamber two. If you look at them we're on the right and people always start from the left. Surely group one should be first. Maybe two is the pale lady's lucky number. Maybe she alternates or flips a coin to amuse herself, but of all the outrages being executed isn't the greatest. Execution is just cruelty, vengeance, the unrestrained use of power. Those things are easy to understand. It's the arbitrariness that's unfathomable, knowing that the twenty of us packed so closely in here will be gasping for breath, then hanging dead in our harnesses, while the lucky number ones are breathing easily with minutes more to live. Can't we just know why?

We were on the bus less than ten minutes ago.

I was in the shower less than two hours ago.

My lawyer told me not to hold my breath less than a month ago.

But at least there's no acid after, no fire. There won't be respect, no coffin, no shroud, and we'll probably all end up a jumble of bodies in the same unmarked hole, then bones, but at least there'll be something left of me, somewhere.

Is it too much to ask for a broken valve? A short circuit? A faulty wire? But that won't happen. The government threw money at the problem of slow executions. It's far less expensive to build fast and robust killing equipment and use it often than to build more prison cells to hold the condemned. And two gas chambers with a common wall is no accident. I'm sure the equipment for each can operate the other, ensuring complete redundancy. When prisoners are shuttled into these metal boxes corpses come out.

The sound of the machinery beneath us isn't loud, but it gets our full attention. It sounds like it's just under the chamber floor. There are hydraulic actuators and electric motors, the faint tick of mechanical relays opening or closing. Each does whatever it's supposed to do to make things ready, then there's a pause, an interminable pause, probably only a second or two long, but it's so deliberate it's unbearable. The thought of the pale lady sitting at her controls, her delicate hands making it all happen so carefully, makes my blood run colder than when she touched me. The unmistakable sound of a large solenoid retracting is so sharp, so loud, it clears every thought from my head. It's ominous, menacing. Another follows, and then all is silent. Those were the final sounds. The machine is ready. I don't know how I know, but I know those solenoids activating were the final step in the preparations. The sounds repeat to our left, but softer, and the two solenoids firing there somehow seem even more terminal. The other chamber is ready.

Now it's our turn again.

We wait.

The next sound will be the fans, then gas flooding our chamber.

Can they just do this? Can she? Push a button and

twenty people locked in a brutalist steel box vanish forever with no more effort than turning on a washing machine? Life and death determined by the push of a button. And that's it? We're gone, hanging dead and limp, ready for the dirt? Then she repeats the motions and the people next to us meet the same fate?

A faint hissing sound sends a wave of panic surging through the chamber. No warning, no ceremony, just the hiss of compressed gas being released, a sound that makes us jerk in our bonds, generating waves that ripple through our connected flesh from one end of the chamber to the other and back.

I hold my breath. I'm not going to do this. I can't do this. I don't want to be the change.

Please.

A handful of seconds later muffled screams, horrified and shocked, come through the shared wall of our chambers. It's the most beautiful sound I've ever heard, a choir of angels heralding a miracle. It's beyond a miracle. The pale lady is processing group one first. I know the twenty people whose death machine has been activated probably feel as cheated as they are surprised —two goes first. We always go first. They expected to hear our panicked cries just as we expected to be making them, but the elation that crashes through our chamber is real—a dusty farmer dropping to his knees in a downpour after a soil fracturing drought, a sailor mad with thirst sighting lush green land at the mouth of a river after a month in a lifeboat mocked by water that would kill him if he succumbed to temptation. I don't care how selfish and heartless it is, I don't feel sorry for them. I want them to scream and scream and scream. It was them or us, and so much better them than us—so much better. In a few minutes they won't exist anymore and we will, and it's beautiful. I don't know why the pale lady chose them and I don't care. I don't care that when she finishes with them she'll do the same to us. What's important is that right now she's monitoring and adjusting the gas saturation levels for them, and it feels incredible. I take a long, slow, deep, easy breath. It feels like deliverance.

But the elation is short lived.

The shocked and terrified screams are replaced by a chorus of insistent, frightened, even angry begging, and pleas for mercy. They're impassioned, desperate, trying to convey their message to an audience of one just outside their box who's doubtless listening to them as intently as we are, but with professional interest, waiting until just the right moment to silence them forever.

Their individual voices are unintelligible, part of a torrid, frothy whole that's greater than the sum of its parts, human fused with animal, expressing desperation, rage, terror, and hopelessness, all riding a wave of disbelief, as if they thought they could just will their fate away. More disturbing is the way the sound evolves, morphing in ways that make it seem like a strange exotic animal caught in a trap. At first it's a snarl, then a whimper, and finally a ghostly wailing, sometimes flipping back to a previous incarnation almost instantly, sometimes flowing slowly one into another, but with every change the volume fades, the number of people emoting simultaneously lessens, until finally individual words sometimes rise above the din —'God,' 'Help,' and, 'No,' are the most emphatic, with an occasional increasingly pathetic, 'Please,' and choked disbelieving moans audible between surges. I don't know how long it's been, a minute? Two at the most, and I find myself wondering why she doesn't do it—increase the gas and end it. I just want them to be quiet. After what seems like forever the noise ebbs, like a tide receding, the sounds getting softer, the occasional crescendos choppier, more widely spaced, more pathetic, until finally there's blessed silence.

I'm not sure if I blinked through that whole thing, and I'm glad it's over, but now I feel sorry for them, and hate myself for feeling elation I couldn't control, but at least I'm still feeling something. And honestly, would any of them have felt differently if those horrible sounds were coming from our chamber, if they were listening? And how would empathy have helped them? They still would have screamed. They still would have begged until they couldn't beg anymore. They'd still be dead and slumped in their harnesses, or dying. The pale lady said something about dealing with dying brains and spontaneous breaths and how it takes a few minutes, and that's all we have left barring another miracle, so why should I feel bad that I didn't feel bad? I didn't condemn those people, and I certainly couldn't have helped them. Would they have felt warm fuzzies coming through a steel wall? Would they have felt better if they thought I was so shocked by their pathetic struggles that I would have sent a strongly worded letter to the editor if I wasn't locked in an identical chamber awaiting exactly the same thing?

And despite the terror flowing from them this exercise isn't about fear. It has nothing to do with punishment. It's about control. It's about who determines who has the freedom to speak, and to act, and who has the ability to say who must be silenced, who must vanish. And somehow we ended up doing something intolerable to the people with the power to make those decisions. And I want to believe those noises weren't triggered by terror and pain, but merely anxiety—confused people having to deal with the reality of nonexistence overtaking them. I want to believe the pale lady is right. Maybe it is just like running a race, getting winded, not being able to catch your breath then, 'out like a light...' forever.

And, horrifying as this chamber is, being locked in such a small space, unable to move, pressed between two naked strangers except for the harnesses that bind us, awaiting nothingness—it's not uncomfortable. I could compare it to a crowded subway at rush hour, but it's not apt. Subways are crowded, claustrophobic, you're locked in a metal box, but there the similarities end. The subway is chaos and confusion. This is order and purpose. This is bright and clean and warm—and now blessedly quiet. With the strange way the harnesses support us it splays our legs and pulls them forward just a bit so we fit together spoon style—chest pressed to back, pelvis front to pelvis back, front of thighs to back of thighs, and we wait.

There is no clock.

The shadows don't move.

There hasn't been a sound from outside our chamber since the voices stopped. There's no way to tell how much time has elapsed, but anxiety affects your perception of time. You'd think it would race, that it would all happen too soon, but it seems like more than a few minutes have elapsed, that all of group one must be well and truly and irrevocably dead, that it must surely be our turn, but the seconds keep ticking benignly by. Maybe something is happening, but what? Has some piece of hardware failed? That seems unlikely. I haven't heard any machinery under us since what must have been the fail-safes releasing. No, this machine is primed and ready, a rocket on the launch pad, its twenty travelers strapped in for a one-way trip out of existence, the clock at T minus some number and counting—towards a zero that will come as a horrific surprise.

But one thing is certain, the air is getting stale, so maybe it's not an illusion. And then a thought occurs— has the woman I'm pressed against actually gotten her reprieve? If she has will the rest of us be given clemency? They can't very well open the chamber, slide us out, take her down, then seal us back in and let the pale lady process us, can they? Not after what we had to listen to. It would be unbelievably cruel to

66

shuttle us into the chamber again, to have to hear the door seal, the machinery primed, knowing not just what it does, but how it affects the people it's doing it to. Maybe they're working out the details. Maybe they'll leave us in here until they can get the bus back. Maybe they're sending for clothes, will send us home directly from here, more likely we'll get a life of incarceration so we can't divulge what we've seen—heard, but I'd rather spend seventy years in prison than five minutes in here.

The longer the wait the better the news. I'm sure we're all thinking along the same lines, but won't tempt fate by saying it out loud. Another minute drags by, maybe two. And then I think—maybe the reprieve is mine. Maybe somebody watched the videos of my arrest, realized I didn't do anything wrong. Maybe I'm getting a pardon, or at least a new trial. Why shouldn't it be my miracle? And even if I'm the only one spared, well, it would be horrible, but I'd sign whatever they wanted me to sign, live wherever they wanted me to live, and you can be damn sure I'd never speak a word about what I saw here, what I heard, far too afraid of a return journey to ever utter a syllable. And while the others, even the pregnant lady, would probably fade, No Fear would live on quietly, ridiculously, as electrical impulses in my brain for another forty years, maybe more, with her dyed skin, desperate tattoos, and mousy squeaks.

"I'm sorry for the wait." It's the pale lady's voice coming through the intercom, as calm and pleasant as

67

before. "It usually doesn't take this long, but it can't be helped. We have a couple of holdouts in the first chamber, hearts that are still giving erratic spasms, trying to restart, and I'll have to give them the full five minutes after the last one stops to be sure cardiac arrest is irreversible. I know it's getting stuffy in there, but I can't open a door. What's coming isn't gas, so don't be frightened. I'm going to inject some air to make you more comfortable. I know the wait is stressful, but I promise I'll process you as soon as I can."

Despite the warning the sharp hissing noise makes everyone jump. My heart races, but the air in the chamber cools and freshens almost instantly, and I'm honestly grateful for it despite my crushed hopes, but it's also terrifying because the gas must come in just as fast, must make the atmosphere toxic as quickly as the air makes it fresh, which explains the wave of terror that swept through chamber one so quickly when their processing began.

A few moments later her voice comes through the speaker again. "Only one to go now. It's erratic, but we have to wait for it to stop."

Is it the pregnant lady's? Is the monitor detecting something inside her? Does a fetus suffocate more slowly than its mother? Does it cling to its unlived life more dearly?

Whatever it was, it's gone, finished—the soft hissing of the gas being injected into their chamber again is final, chilling, the pale lady immersing them in pure carbon dioxide to extinguish any miracle spark that

tries to reignite life. I know it's over; I know they're
dead, but there's a horrible finality about that sound.
Somehow erasing any last chance for revival seems an
act of abject cruelty, not the mercy the pale lady tried to
laminate it with. It does, however, erase any question
about her resolve, about our future. In fifteen or twenty
seconds the sound stops, leaving us in horrible silence,
heralding the start of our five minute timer as it begins
ticking towards eternity unseen. I suppose when all
hope is gone all you have is fantasy. Experts say that's
how religions are born. I'd like to think there's
something beyond this chamber, believe something
more than pigs being ushered into gas chambers right
now on the first leg of their trip to meat counters where
their lives will be reduced to the streaks of fat running
through their thin sliced belly musculature, judged by
customers who'll select a winner through clear
clingfilm covered bacon trays to sizzle in their frying
pans, but I don't want heaven, don't need choirs of
winged angels, human or porcine, a marble kingdom in
the clouds filled with ethereal song and fractious
squealing. I just want normalcy, some way to get this
horrible tattooed lady back into her overpriced leotard
so I can try to get her out of it and get my hands on her
soft, bare ass instead of having my pelvis shoved
against it. I want to thrust my uncertainty and regrets
away, fill her with seed that will never fertilize an egg
so I can be disgusted by her all over again, disgusted by
everything about her except her amazing blue eyes, so
pretty I'd tell her I'd die for them, but never would;

surely those are worth saving, by someone. They have to be. Something has to be worth saving otherwise all we have is this horrible numbness, this sweating skin covering spongy organs attached to frangible skeletons, this invisible timer that must be approaching zero.

The chamber plunges into absolute blackness without warning, an inky blanket not a pinprick of light penetrates. It's punctuated by half a dozen stifled yelps and gasps the darkness seems to induce and cancel simultaneously. Tensed muscles send a single ripple through connected flesh like it's no longer part of any individual. My breathing is shallow, but my heart beats hard against my sternum, so hard I think it may be trying to break through my rib cage. It's so black I can't be sure I've ever seen anything, so complete I don't know if I've ever had eyes. I press my fingertips into No Fear's smooth warm skin, take comfort in feeling the outline of her wide feminine pelvis beneath it, and try not to picture the corpses in the next chamber hanging in the same lightless void we're trapped in, heads and limbs limp, eyes wide and empty. I never imagined their desperate sounds emanating from such utter blackness, and their silence now seems both admonition and mocking invitation.

I can't believe the pale lady is contemplating the same fate for us even if she does this every day. She spoke to me, her voice softer, kinder than any I've encountered since my arrest, yet in my mind's eye a black tipped finger rests on a red button until I force my visualization lower and see her bright bare calves pressed together tense and ladylike knee to ankle, see her polished heels hooked over the gleaming chrome footrest ringing the bottom of her chair, pivoting her feet so her toes, bared by two narrow intersecting straps that make up the entirety of her shoes' uppers, point down precariously, as much warning as promise.

The soft sound of the circulation fans is like a sledgehammer to the psyche as the air in our chamber begins moving at the pace of the gentlest summer breeze. Like hunted animals we freeze; we don't make a sound; we hardly breathe, and for moment after moment the danger stays at bay, until the pressure becomes too much for the woman whose warm hips are so comforting. They twitch. I try to calm her with a little squeeze, but her panicked voice erupts, filling the chamber like thunder. She begins stammering, "They're dead. They're all dead. Somebody stop her. Make her turn on the lights. I want to see. I don't like this. I want to see. I want to go home. This isn't fair. I..."

Her stream of consciousness is interrupted by a piercing hiss and disruption in the chamber's atmosphere.

"Stop," she screams, her voice tearing, her body convulsing against mine. "You can't."

The rest of us hold our breaths. Between forced hope and stabbing fear, while the hiss and rush might still be anything, another feeling, base and destructive, rises from the darkness, pride—pride that the pale lady's pushed the button, pride that she's demonstrating her power, pride that she's putting us in our place so effortlessly with her perfect manicure, perfect pedicure, perfect lipstick, her attentive eyes focused on her instruments so professionally. And if they built all this for us, if she came here for us, then we must deserve it, then we should embrace it, but still we hold our breaths and hope it hasn't started.

Given the chance I think we'd all spend eternity overwhelmed by this moment, but time is still shoving us remorselessly forward, second by bitter second and, as if given a cue, as if will and reason never existed, we all seem to take a tentative breath simultaneously. Carbon dioxide may be odorless and colorless, but it has a mass and feel, and a tasteless taste that sits on the tongue that's instantly, horribly apparent. Disbelief shatters and the chamber fills with screams—no, one scream, one terrified, outraged scream coming from a chorus of individual voices, pathetic despite its earsplitting volume. For a moment I think I'm an observer, then I feel the vibrations in my own throat and realize I'm part of the choir, twenty voices tenuously attached to our souls making terror audible. Almost before I recognize it, it shifts—the begging begins, the unbearable thoughts becoming tremulous words. The woman ahead of me is the only one I can make out. "Not me, please. I'm good. I'm good. Help me, I'm...."

My lungs are empty. I hold my breath as long as I can until my body overrides my will and takes a deep breath of the horrible mixture. It instantly makes my need for air even more desperate. The suggestion to relax and breathe deeply now seems like a cruel joke. No one can willingly inhale whatever the pale lady's immersed us in. "Stop. You have to stop," I cry into the cacophonous desperation making the walls ring. This isn't anything like she described. My lungs are filled with something heavy and noxious that makes the need to breathe overpowering. I snatch another breath of the horror involuntarily and it makes it worse again, so much worse. I try to hold my breath, but the need for air is irresistible. This can't be how it's supposed to happen. Something has gone horribly wrong. "Dear God, stop, please stop," I choke into the blackness, not sure if I'm praying to an almighty I don't believe in or a woman who's no more than eight feet away from me, but our distorted prayers have the same effect on her that our counterparts' did as they futilely struggled for lives she so skillfully extracted from them. It can't end for us like it ended for them, a blind chorus screaming pathetically into the void. This can't be another routine processing, like the one before, like the ones to follow, two or three minutes of discordant noise followed by an eternity of silence, it can't.

Our pressed bodies undulate as we struggle blind in our harnesses for impossible escape, one mass of flesh forced together moving like a single mindless thing. I take another breathless breath that leaves me more desperate and beg again, "Help us, help. It's not like you said," but my words vanish into the cacophony, and as they do I realize to my horror that I'm erect, that my penis is pressed against the smooth warm back of the

73

woman with the No Fear tattoo, that the nipples of the woman whose sweaty breasts are pressed against my back are now like two pebbles, and despite the horrific atmosphere we're drowning in that seems to distort every sense, it can't hide the subtle pheromone laced smell that tells me that some, perhaps all the women here, are sharing in this confused excitement, awaiting stimulation they'll never get suspended as they are, but the constant writhing as we struggle in the blackness quickly brings me towards climax. And then I realize— this, too, is supposed to happen. It's just another part of a routine processing, the messy aftermath of which the pale and bronze ladies have seen hundreds of times. When I imagined the corpses in the chamber next to us hanging motionless in their harnesses they were the decorous, dignified dead cocooned in the pale lady's shining steel altar, sacrifices almost holy. I never envisioned erections, hard nipples, open and engorged sexes. I never imagined viscous semen or animal lubricant dripping onto the spotless polished metal floor of that chamber, all of which will be scrubbed clean by knowing hands before new arrivals see it to make sure it comes as a surprise for them, too.

Belief is a strange and illogical thing, as is its opposite, and everything in between. The pale lady's job is to kill us. Her goal is to kill us. She told us exactly how she's going to kill us. She's set the machinery to kill us in motion, but somehow I still don't believe she wants for us what she did to them. It can't be. The hissing begins again. She's injecting more gas. She can't—that's the one thing she can't do. I pull at my bonds, try to struggle out of the harness, but the straps bind like iron, seem to be getting tighter, testing my ribs, testing my spine. I'm dizzy, falling, spinning slowly down. "Somebody stop her," I beg, but I can barely make out my own words, and the voices around me are getting softer, not as emphatic, but are just as desperate. The woman behind me is whimpering rhythmically between gasps, but her nipples feel like they're eroding the skin of my back. "Somebody please..." she repeats several times at intervals, her voice plain, genuine, confused.

My deep choking rasps devolve into panting and my lungs burn, but my arousal grows as if to spite me. I need release. I need relief, but I can't control the rhythm of the single fleshy thing the twenty of us have devolved into in the blackness, none of us can. The undulations are organic, wavelike, less like twenty people struggling for their lives, or for pleasure, more like an undulating marine flatworm burrowing into lethal sea mud to die for reasons known only to it.

"God... God...," a man's voice somewhere ahead of me stammers, his voice barely louder than mine, and I know he's ejaculating. My eyes open wide in the blackness. I'm on the brink, almost go over. I clench my teeth. She can't want this, can't see this. I can't stop the processing, but I can stop this. It may not be worse than death, but would certainly be the most humiliating insult that could be added to it, make it look like I enjoyed the experience when they pull my corpse out, make it look like I've given the pale lady a final salute for a job well done, for lipstick perfectly applied. Yet I can't erase the vision of her delicate hands on the controls she's orchestrating this all with, the soft white skin in such contrast to her gleaming black nails. I see her moistening her lips with the tip of her tongue. Somebody goes home to those lips, kisses them, and when he asks how her day was, what does she say? Does she proudly tell him the nature of the passions she unleashes inside this box as we struggle in vain, laughing when she does, or merely hint at it with a sidelong glance and a little smile? And does he praise her for it as he takes her hand and guides her to the bedroom? No, I can't allow her to distill this nightmare into an aphrodisiac to fuel their lust, don't want her to fashion uncontrollable reflex into a sacrifice consecrating their flesh coupling rite as I'm being reduced to a depraved memory that will be erased when the next group of the condemned discover what she's capable of. But I can't stop her, can't slow her, and fall helplessly when those hands drop me head first into the gaping maw of a formless sable dark predator that swallows me whole, and I sink spinning into its warm wet gullet where slow, slippery, rippling contractions draw me inexorably towards its strange oblivion.

By the time I snap back the horrifying reality is upon me. "No, please..." I beg, "not like this... not like this," but I'm past the point of no return. I gasp and implode. I flail and thrash against it in my bonds, against everything it stands for, futilely. It's turning me inside out, liquefying me, each pulsation so intense it's like they're being wrung from me bodily one excruciating contraction at a time by delicate black nailed fingers, more pain than pleasure, and having it happen inside this death machine makes a cruel mockery of its life-giving highest purpose, and the sensation of my wasted semen churning pathetic and hot between my body and the tattooed woman's is vile, disgusting, and as inescapable as this harness, this chamber, but somehow, somehow, it's no more than we deserve.

I want to live this shame silently then dissolve into the soft encompassing flesh, but a torrid moan gurgles unstoppable from the back of my throat so loud that outside the pale lady must hear it, can't mistake it for anything other than what it is. There must be a little smile gently tugging at the edges of her soft pink lips, a knowing glance exchanged with her grinning assistant, and I pray she'll be satisfied with the sound, that it won't pique her interest, trigger an inspection when I'm hanging lifeless—and another more intimate judgment that will reduce my life to a gooey mess thickening on a stranger's back, but if she can't resist looking, either in pride or amusement, I hope she'll show us the courtesy of washing it away after her curiosity's been satisfied, letting the water run until it's fresh and clear before burial. I'm pulsing empty, feel like a squeezed orange, a spongy husk, and the pain is worse; it's like pulp and pits being forced through my urethra with each wringing spasm until finally, mercifully, it subsides into a series of throbbing raw palpitations before they, too, finally ebb, then stop with an echoing finality that's more like death than the one the pale lady is so calmly inflicting on me.

The exertion has left me panting like a dog, breath after intolerable breath, each adding to the carbon dioxide that's poisoning my blood instead of cleansing it, forcing me down the chamber's devious death spiral towards oblivion with ever increasing speed. I desperately want to live, but each time I try to hold my breath and buy myself a few more seconds of hellacious consciousness my body betrays me. When I manage to quell the panting for a moment or two it ends with a rasping gasp and my lungs fill and burn like I'm inhaling molten sulfur, which leaves me panting faster and deeper than before, and my heart pounding like it's been clamped in a paint shaker.

I don't want to be the first to fall limp. I can't be first. I want to beg again, but my lungs are pumping too fast to speak. My mind seems to start and stop with jerks. I can't struggle anymore, but the squirming of the others keeps me moving, soft sweaty flesh yielding to soft sweaty flesh that feels like it's melting together. The human sounds around me are fading, and the only constant is the patient hiss of the gas injectors slowly raising the CO_2 levels to the point where first consciousness, then life, is impossible. I try to scream an ear shattering, 'Help,' one last time in hopes that maybe in the relative quiet the pale lady will hear me, but it's barely a gasp.

How many times has she done this? Is it too much to

ask that just once she gives a reprieve? Can't we be the exception that makes the rule? Can't the chamber door open just once and relieved, happy, grateful people unable to control their emotions emerge? And if she won't stop it can she give us a small gift, an instant's mercy, inject another minute's air before finishing the job? Can't she understand what a minute's life means to people seconds from eternal nothingness? What can it matter to her? She's radiant, beautiful. She's no monster. She spoke to me.

I'm spinning faster, falling faster. With all my strength, amidst growing confusion and all encompassing fear, I force my body to stop gasping for just a moment and try to beg her for help again. I stammer, "Thank you," but it's barely a whisper. For an instant I'm elated I spoke, then failure turns in on me. My head jerks erect. I nearly slipped into unconsciousness. I can't lose consciousness. Lose consciousness, 'And that's it. It's over for you,' she warned. It's a one way trip, 'Nobody wakes up.' They probably have a hole dug already... Her calves... I don't want her to put me in a hole... Her lips... I don't want to rot in the ground... Her hands... My head jerks upright again. Her... One last chance, one word, 'Help,' one word, loud, one word. Make her hear it. She has to save you. She will save you. But it has to happen now... It has to happen now... It has to... "Bacon," I whisper into the void as I feel my head fall forward.

Part II

The chamber's been silent for more than half a minute. Their futile panic and passions spent, my customers are either unconscious or hovering happily in a dreamlike state close to it. One by one they've accepted their fate, surrendered to the carbon dioxide, and are letting it do its job without resistance. I began adjusting the gas mix as soon as their voices faded, bringing the CO_2 concentration up to the kill level slowly. Some may argue that it was a touch too soon, that you should wait longer then use a heavier hand, but this is more art than science, and there's always a trade off between speed and the customers' anxiety and discomfort, which can only be mitigated, not eliminated. I generally opt for just a bit faster unconsciousness with a bit more discomfort, but that's a matter of preference and varies from executioner to executioner. Some even go strictly by time, though personally I think they're taking the easy way out. When the CO_2's holding steady at a hair over twenty-two percent, my special Goldilocks mixture that triggers maximum respiration for rapid oxygen displacement guaranteed to be lethal, I switch my attention to the panel's heart rate displays, cross my legs, and watch. They're all at a hundred eighty to two hundred beats per minute, give or take, doing their final sprint towards eternity for me. Several are no longer in sinus rhythm. They're about to start falling like dominoes, one flat line after another, and this is always the most satisfying part of the job for me, because it's what this whole enterprise is about—the end. I won't say it's better than sex, but it's as good in its own way. Given the choice between a day processing customers and a night being ravaged by my husband I'd choose the one I hadn't just experienced.

And there goes the first one, near the middle of the screen, and I even know who it is—the curious boy with the faulty monitor. I'm glad he gave it up for me first. We had that little moment, and though he was a little shy, like an eager virgin he seemed genuinely interested—in the equipment, in the procedures, in everything, and even if he was too nervous to look me in the eye I know he was hanging on my every word, absorbing what I told him like a sponge. Most of my customers don't seem to care at all. They're generally content to just let it surprise them. Maybe that's the way they deal with it, but I think it's indicative of a greater societal problem—people just aren't concerned, even about things that affect them intimately. If I didn't know what I know and was about to end up in one of those chambers I hope I'd take more interest than a tiny eyed pig walking into a pork processing plant.

By habit, I always do everything with group two first. There's no real reason for it, probably because when looking at a transport ready to unload group two is on my left and people naturally go left to right, left to right, even if it seems odd to new trainees when I turn around and face the chambers—but that's what I did today, like every day, group two, group one, group two, group one, right up until it came time to actually start processing, and I came incredibly close to doing group two, my curious boy's, first, like normal. We'd had our moment and he was safely flesh swaddled in his chamber and ready to process with the rest of his group and I was quite looking forward to it, if I'm honest, because no other customer had ever thanked me before, and that gratitude meant nothing until he was on his way to nothingness for me, soul and body. I set all the controls, primed the system, released the safeties, and put my finger on the button that would have turned off the lights in chamber two, came so close to pushing it —and if I had my epiphany after I wouldn't have stopped. I'd have turned on the circulation fans, counted to ten quite slowly to let its occupants get accustomed to the darkness, and then I would have processed them as usual—because I wouldn't want to subject any customer to any part of the procedure twice, and besides, this is as much my experience as theirs. I get to savor their anticipation, and I think my excitement must be as great as theirs, but inverted, their yin to my yang, and as it grows the feeling of control morphs into something incredibly zen-like. In those seconds between anticipation and reality it's like the button to inject the gas becomes a part of me, or I a part of it. I don't choose to push it. It's as if some greater subconscious, made of me, the machine, and the customers trapped within it, collectively decide it's time, and the button and I move together, organically, the resultant click and hiss a surprise to us all. It's such a liberating experience, and when I hear my customers' excited reactions to their first few carbon dioxide enriched breaths I get the feeling that all is right with the world, and it transforms me into a virtuoso playing the most sublime instrument ever devised.

And it wouldn't have been a tragedy if I'd processed my curious boy's group first. He certainly never would have known the difference, and the actual processing experience would have been much the same for him, which, if I'm honest, is probably worse than running a race because nobody can run fast enough to raise their blood CO2 to the point where they pass out, but all the customers find that out eventually, so there's no reason to raise their anxiety levels because it won't change anything for them. The only practical difference is that it would have ended twelve or thirteen minutes sooner, and I can't imagine that would have made any difference to him—but I wasn't giving him more time. I was giving him a richer experience, a fuller understanding, and that's what the curious want.

So I processed chamber one.

And that was his gift—letting him listen to it from the outside before experiencing it directly for himself from within, because I knew he might not be able to appreciate the nuances of the evolving sounds when he was part of the chorus making them, especially if they came as a surprise, and he certainly wouldn't have been able to savor the quiet at the end, and the quiet is essential; without it you don't really understand the beauty of the finality of it all—and when it was final for the others I processed his group. They were a bit feisty at the start, not unusual for the second chamber because they know what's coming, but that's just blind panic, and a slight boost in the initial CO_2 levels adjusted their attitudes nicely. And I hope that despite the unease and discomfort he must have felt from that first inrush of gas when he had to accept that, yes, this is really happening, to him, and right now, until the moment oblivion took him, that he was able to, if not actually enjoy the experience, at least on some intellectual level, then appreciate the fear, the loss of control, and accept that the process is a continuum which doesn't allow for any other outcome.

The other nineteen dominoes fall in less than thirty seconds—no holdouts. It's not that I don't respect them, those whose hearts beat faintly minutes after their chamber-mates have expired, like those in chamber one earlier. They're probably unconscious, but you've got to admire their bodies' tenacity for fighting the losing fight, for hanging on long after the others have been reduced to a light lunch for the vats, but it's always more satisfying to see a group surrender almost simultaneously, like they're saluting me for a job well done. I increase the CO2 level in their chamber to one hundred percent as fast as the equipment can operate. It takes less than twenty seconds, and will extinguish any spark of life almost instantly if some random neuron in a dying brain fires and one of them takes a spasmodic breath, but none do. Not one inhalation, not a single electrical impulse from their hearts. Their five minutes is up, brain and body death complete, irreversible.

"Clean sweep, boss?" Sunny asks as I engage the safeties and shut down the system.

"Twenty more door-nails," I tell her.

"Sweet," she tells me, extending her vowels in that peculiar way she does when she's happy. "Better to snuff twenty candles than to risk their light."

She's been my assistant for almost two years, and has such a refreshing way of looking at the world. I call her Sunny because of her bright personality and love of the outdoors, which she brings inside with a glowing tan and positive work ethic. While I have had a couple of long term assistants who were extremely good at their jobs and tireless workers, for them it was about the challenges, the excitement, even the power. Sunny, on the other hand, is passionate, but understands passion, in this context, is the desire to process all customers assigned to us cleanly and efficiently, no matter who they are, no matter what they've done, and most importantly, no matter what they haven't done. A good executioner doesn't care about good or bad, guilt or innocence, left or right. That's the purview of those who condemn them, those who initiate reforms. The executioner's job is to make sure they're destroyed without fanfare, without prejudice, and takes satisfaction in that, and Sunny does, that she does it with a broad smile and buoyant personality makes it so much the better.

Trainees who come to me sometimes ask how I'd feel if I found out someone I executed was innocent, and I have to tell them—wonderful, absolutely wonderful, because I know if they ended up in one of my gas chambers they got a good clean relatively quick exit with acceptable amounts of anxiety and discomfort, over in a few minutes, something nature and fate don't guaranty. Sometimes I think it's the innocent who should be executed, that the real punishment is condemning someone to a random death which may happen in their sleep after a perfect day at the end of a wonderful life when they're ready to go, but may also inflict months or years of agony on someone just starting, or in the middle of their life, for no reason anyone can explain. And the truth is most of my customers have been condemned for things that weren't even crimes before the reforms, and I'm guessing their judges would be hard pressed to explain why they should even have been investigated without using words like 'greater good,' and 'danger to democracy,' and 'existential threat.' Their sentences are passed with words like 'menace,' 'turpitude,' and 'deplorable,' but we can't define the justifications—those are ideas, abstractions. Our job is making those abstractions reality, and without emotion, treating arriving customers like animals at a slaughterhouse where incensed squealing pigs, stretched teat milkers too tired to moo, and excited little white lambs that can't resist happily jumping and vocalizing for every new face, all receive the same professional care regardless of whether they're destined for glittering starred restaurants or rust belt fertilizer plants, and Sunny knows this, feels it, which is why she'll make a great executioner when she's ready, probably sooner than later, though it will mean I'll need to find a new assistant, and that can be a real challenge.

"Disposal time?" she asks, reading my mind.

"Disposal time," I reply, getting up from the console. "Bring the tablet," I instruct, but it's already in her hand as we walk around to the other end of the chambers.

Sunny doesn't ask about my changing the processing order. She probably thinks it's because of the pregnant woman in group one. There's an old superstition in the business that processing an expectant mother brings good luck. The rationale is that since executioners take life, the more life they take the more portentous the kill, and if you can take a life before any of it's been lived it's a slam-dunk, the *non plus ultra* of the trade. The

87

man I apprenticed under absolutely swore by it, and would rub their bulging bellies three times clockwise slowly before loading them for even more luck. It's pretty fuzzy logic, but you can kind of see where it's coming from. The reality is probably a bit more practical. We're salaried, and paid well, but we also get a nice little bonus for every customer we process. While we can't get a 'two-fer' with a pregnant lady— no birth, no personhood, obviously, but the reforms do allow us to claim a smaller fee for performing a *de facto* abortion, not a lot, but enough for some of life's little niceties. It makes it worthwhile to check the medical records of all the women sent for processing just to be sure none slip by expectant without showing, and you get pretty good at telling the fat ones from the bonus material by the shape of their bellies. And I just don't get the whole, 'My baby, save my baby,' or some variant thereof they always whine when they find out it's time. I mean, I do my best to calm them with some incredibly elongated truths because they're in real distress and I like to think I'm a nice person, and I am getting more money for no extra work, but sometimes I get so tired of it and just want to say, 'You don't have a baby. You have a fetus. It's part of your body, and that body's been condemned, so I'm not saving your damned baby anymore than I'm saving your damned windpipe, and while both might be interesting to see in jars in my curio cabinet I can only save so much junk.' But I don't. I use platitudes. I tell them they're glowing, or big as a house, and talk to them about their babies getting warm baths, and once they've relaxed a little I can get on with my work, and it's odd that they generally only have the one emotional outburst, that after calming them they remain quiet even when shuttled into a chamber and hearing the order to seal it. Whether they honestly believe the platitudes instead of what they can see, or figure out the absurdity of thinking that having a little carbon copy of themselves inside is going to give them some special privileges, I don't know.

Maybe I'm not very maternal, but I don't even get the whole pregnancy thing—I mean, the idea of a little parasite growing inside me, inflating me like a balloon, ruining my shape, making me walk funny, making me less attractive, maybe even permanently scarring my smooth skin with jagged stretch marks, and then rending my vagina to get out—and there's this little person lying there, wailing, covered in blood and ripped placenta, come to replace me, and I'm supposed to pick it up, hold it to my chest and let it suck life from my tits whenever it wants just so it can grow up and bury me? Talk about something to give you nightmares, which makes me wonder why sex feels so good if that's the intended outcome. And the alternative is even more unattractive to me. It's not that I give a toss about evicting an unwanted guest straight into the medical waste bin, but I don't like the idea of anyone monkeying with my insides, whether that be by jamming a sharp or suction-y tool inside me or using chemicals that some clever lettered scientist figured out would have the same effect if packaged into a pretty little pill and swallowed at the first sign of morning sickness. But I'm pretty good at managing my birth control, though I'll admit that when I get amorous I become distracted and have had the occasional slip-up. Luckily I've been lucky those times, and with luck I'll continue to be—lucky.

"Open disposal door, chamber two." The locking mechanism retracts with a metallic click, and the chamber unseals with a crisp little hiss like the sound of a carbonated beverage can opening. Though the chambers are pressure balanced, we keep processing pressure higher than normal atmospheric pressure, not enough to cause the customers discomfort, but high enough to ensure quick tissue saturation when the gas concentrations are changed resulting in fast biological response, so when I had to bump up the levels in two it only took seconds to quiet them down to nominal volume. You develop a feel for when you need to make adjustments, and how much to make, and that's all Sunny needs. She knows the equipment, the procedures, the mechanics, and she's watching and learning.

The door swings wide slowly and I feel the cool carbon dioxide as it pours over my feet and ankles in refreshing little waves. That's the beauty of CO_2 chambers, not only are they reliable, efficient, inexpensive, and reasonably quick and humane, but there's no need to neutralize any nasty chemicals, or even flush the chamber before opening. Though it was at one hundred percent concentration its volume is so small compared to the processing room that what was so terrifying to its occupants a few minutes ago simply flows invisibly and harmlessly away along the floor.

The man at the front of the chamber is still erect, and the inside of the disposal door is splashed with several distinct jets of thickening semen seeping down it slowly. This isn't unusual. Executioners have been documenting the sexual response of their customers to execution for centuries, some going so far as to differentiate, and record by name, the prisoners who only achieved erection from those who actually ejaculated, but it's something the public only whispers about because it makes them uncomfortable—execution is fine, more than fine, many are enthusiastic about it, but arousal or orgasm during execution is taboo, somehow makes a pure rite sordid. It's perfectly natural, though. Sexual response to stress, fear, and danger are all well documented, as is sexual response to a lack of oxygen and buildup of carbon dioxide, which is why choke sex, while dangerous, is a very real thing. Virtually everyone who ends up in one of my chambers shows some degree of arousal when they're removed. Whether it was enjoyable for them is a matter of conjecture, though I'd like to think you couldn't have an experience like that and not feel some pleasure, and gratitude for the person who triggered it.

I'd guess that on average about three quarters of the men I process ejaculate, or at least leak significant quantities of seminal fluid, and since sex organs stay frozen in the condition they are at the time of death, and they're often quite rigid despite having ejaculated, it shows that they achieved orgasm almost immediately before cardiac arrest. Similar numbers of women are clearly aroused, but there's no way to tell if they achieved release. Stimulation is easier for men because their genitals are always pressed against someone, or against the door like the lead man in the chamber, and their struggles usually provide enough direct stimulation to trigger release, though I have a feeling it must be a bitter pill for a man in front to be making love to the machine that's killing him. The nature of the harnesses, which pull the legs apart to provide comfortable suspension by spreading most of the weight between the fleshy inner thighs and lower buttocks, prevents women from rubbing directly against anything most of the time, though I suppose with enough motion some of them do achieve relief, at least it would be nice if they did. I know the harnesses can be redesigned to rectify this, a center strap bisecting the sex with a knurled insert of appropriate material should be enough to make even a frigid customer ring the bell on her way out, and I'm sure the bureau would implement any suggestion I made if worded appropriately. The review committee certainly wouldn't approve a harness change to allow women to orgasm during processing. That would be tawdry, but they'd approve it in a heartbeat if the change 'comforted,' or 'eased distress.' It's not that its members are naive. They'd see the design and instantly know what the change would achieve, the men with relish, women with a cool thrill, but it wouldn't actually be approved pruriently. That's merely the internalization, and ultimately they really do want to make processing as humane as possible because they tell themselves they're not monsters, so the change would be made with pure heart. But female customers' physical relief, or lack thereof, doesn't affect my interaction with them, so isn't a priority for me, and honestly, I'm happy just to see the artifacts of their arousal. It shows they were distracted. Plus, I'm not sure if satisfaction, or a last failed grab at satisfaction, is more romantic, and most women, especially the kind sent here, are all about the romance; they believe in things—the wrong things for the times, but things nonetheless.

The load was fifty-fifty, ten men, ten women, which I always request, and the reforms made certain that arrests and sentences wouldn't be skewed, that those condemned would be proportionately representative of their makeup of the population in terms of identifiable physical characteristics so as not to discriminate even if it means some more or less innocent people might be accused and some guilty people get overlooked to round out the numbers. Sunny loaded boy-girl, boy-girl, which is my preferred configuration, and this has nothing to do with etiquette or propriety. I find that by having each customer sandwiched between members of the opposite sex it tends to moderate their reactions which I find helpful. When men are pressed against men their aggression can surface, and woman to woman can give rise to sharp tension edged cattiness, both of which can accelerate and amplify their reactions to the gas. Male to female, female to male, mollifies them to a certain extent, puts them on their best behavior, allowing me to make more refined adjustments.

It's not in the bureau's protocol, but then I don't always follow the protocol. Being in charge of your own facility allows a lot of latitude in how you handle things, and it's not that I'm trying to be a maverick. I want to improve the welfare of my customers while they're in my charge. I can't modify the physical building or equipment without permission, but I can use what they supply as I see fit. The 'L' shaped processing area with two chambers 'around the corner' has been adopted as the standard facility configuration since the reforms. It was designed for maximum throughput, and what its designers saw as creating minimum stress for the staff and customers, and to achieve this they tried to maximize speed and minimize information. In a 'by the book' plant customers aren't told what's happening until the last moment. Once a group's conveyor is activated they move non-stop off the bus, around the bend, and into their chamber. It's sealed, the lights are turned off, then the next chamber is loaded, sealed, and darkened. After that they're processed sequentially—total time from bus door opening until gas is injected in the first chamber, about three minutes, with customers learning for certain through the intercom seconds before it begins. And this was all done for a reason—

the turn in the 'L' saves those still on the bus from the stress of seeing the first chamber loaded and sealed, and the empty chamber waiting for them. Loading with the lights on saves customers from being forcibly moved from a lighted place to a darkened one. Indeed, the standard design makes the chamber interior slightly brighter than the room's ambient light level.

Immediately darkening it after it's sealed is thought to have the same effect as putting a towel over a birdcage at night, or turning off the lights in a child's room at bedtime, and there's no doubt that blackening the chamber during processing reduces stress. Humans are visual animals, and if they can't see stressful things, like the other customers reacting to the gas, it will lower their own anxiety as they go through the same thing.

I'm not saying the protocol is wrong, only that my experience suggests ways to make it even easier on our customers at the expense of adding only a few minutes to their journey, something the industry owes them, in my opinion. While it's true that not telling customers of their execution until the very last moment allows them to live in denial, deluding themselves into believing the chambers are some kind of new showers based on the drive-through car wash principle, or high tech medical scanners for arriving prisoners, or whatever else they can dream up other than what they obviously are, if customers only learn what's happening seconds before it begins their panic level goes off the scale, and the way we were taught to do it was pretty brutal, tell them,

"You're being executed, breathe deeply," through the PA speakers, then immediately injecting gas. I was even chided for adding a 'please' between 'executed' and 'breathe' my first time at the controls, my trainer confusing politeness with weakness. My customers didn't make that mistake, though.

It's not that many manage to take it stoically when they find they can't breathe, whether they find out three minutes or three seconds before it starts, but their reactions are somewhat less intense if they have some time to get accustomed to the knowledge, which makes my job of tailoring the gas levels to their reactions more precise. That's why I take just a minute or two to tell them their fate before they see what's waiting for them. The designers also thought that seeing the chambers being loaded would cause undo stress. In my early trial and error days I discovered this isn't the case. What ramps up their anxiety is seeing a chamber door closing with others in it, or seeing a closed chamber knowing others are inside. There seems to be a finality in the closed door that they don't like, and I have to admit they look a bit intimidating. That's why I load both chambers before sealing either. The only customers who can watch them close are towards the rear of their own chamber, and they usually choose not to, staring straight ahead as it happens, though some look back when they hear the sound of the hydraulics, but they usually avert their eyes before the door seals—not that I blame them. And my final deviation from the protocol is to leave the lights on until just before processing.

Turning them off right after loading may serve the purpose they intend, but only until the group going second has to hear those going first from blackness. Heart rate data alone shows they're more relaxed if they listen with the lights on. The clincher is that if both chambers are black the customers in both often start screaming when gas is only flowing to one. I'm sorry, but they just got it wrong on that point, so wrong I've actually tried to get the bureau to change the protocol. I'm sure they eventually will, but government agencies change slowly. Until then, I'll let them have their guidelines, but I'll follow my muse.

I order Sunny to advance group two out of their chamber. I always love this part. It's like my birthday when the cake is gone and it's time to open the gifts. They begin to move with a metallic bang that echos off the steel walls as the twenty conveyor locks release almost simultaneously, after which they slide almost silently out, so close together they're more one mass of flesh than twenty individuals. The looks on most of their faces is a combination of surprise, embarrassment, and exhaustion, but the last few minutes have been pretty rough and they can be excused for not looking shower fresh. I take a good deal of pride in having given them a good, but brief, workout.

I'm sure they didn't think I'd go through with it—we're all the heroes of our own stories, and the hero always makes a miraculous escape—everybody knows that, and because they can't imagine themselves not existing they think others can't, either. Unfortunately for them my imagination is quite good. It doesn't matter that this facility is a temple dedicated to their sacrifice, that the steel womb I locked them in to await de-conception is its *sanctum sanctorum* and horned high altar combined. I bet most, if not all my customers, believe they'll get a last second reprieve, or a show of mercy, so they're surprised first when processing starts, then are shocked, dumbfounded even, when it doesn't stop, that no cavalry charges in to save them, that the machinery operates exactly as designed and extinguishes their lives so efficiently. From the startled sounds coming from within it's obvious they think they can scramble and come up with magic words which will make the gas go away and door open, and scream them with increasing desperation until they can't scream anymore, and if that provides them comfort until they surrender to their desire, then the gas, so much the better, but the truth is I've heard them all before, in more or less the same order, thousands of times, and they've never worked, not even once. They're followed with groans, with gasps, with sighs, with quiet pleading, then silence, every time.

Their vocalizations are useful to me, though, helping me gauge how much gas to inject and when. If they start too loud, like group two did, I give them a bit more to calm them down. If they quiet down abruptly I hold off on raising the levels for a bit. What I'm aiming for is moderate volume at the start with a gently fluctuating fade to silence. I'm not sure if they know they're assisting me, but I doubt it would change

98

anything if they did. They might not want to help, but the panic would get the better of them, which is as good for them as it is for me. If, somehow, they were able to remain silent from beginning to end they might suffer more because I wouldn't be able to tailor the processing to their needs.

I give them a once-over. I'd be lying if I said I didn't enjoy seeing the physical manifestations of their excitement, knowing they were thinking of me in their final passions. Though I'm curious about my curious boy I take my time, giving each corpse its due. They're still tightly packed by the machinery, and this isn't done merely to most efficiently utilize the space available in the chambers. Fitting the customers together spoon style for processing maximizes human contact which both comforts and distracts, so I have to nudge and push to separate them for their final inspection, but the results are perfect so far. Every man shows at least some discharge, most are still fully erect, and every woman has at least moderately engorged nipples and a shiny sex; nearly all are at least partially blooming. The lady expecting a reprieve is, somewhat surprisingly considering her shopworn condition, in full on exotic orchid mode, and the thigh straps at the bottom of her harness are sticky. Though I can't say for sure, if any of the women have gone out happy she has, and not just because of the state of her sex and crinkled nipples, but because her face doesn't just register surprise, but shock, as if she was really experiencing something when she was overcome, possibly for the first time.

Like I said, it's not the goal, but it is flattering.

"Looks like all the customers are satisfied," Sunny tells me, reading my mind.

I finally get to my curious boy, separate him from the orchid woman in front of him, take a good look and chuckle. He's fully erect, painfully, even, and his scrotum is high and tight, gripping his testicles firmly. While his penis is a bit below average, both in length and girth, and tilts up strangely near its end, its swollen mushroom head is an angry deep pink verging on red, and its shaft's veins bulge bluish, but what's truly impressive is the amount of ejaculate he's deposited on the lady's tramp stamp, which itself is impressive. I'd noticed it as she went in the chamber, but hadn't read it. Inside all the, 'I've hit forty and my life is empty so I want to look like a slut,' scroll work it reads, 'No Fear,' which I'm guessing she regretted getting about the time the lights went out, and if she was hoping the curious boy's pressure wash would make it unreadable before anyone saw it she'd be sadly disappointed, but it'll come clean in the wash. It always does.

"I bet she felt that," Sunny observes with a smile, lifting her phone and snapping a picture of the congealing aftermath for posterity before lowering it and getting one of the woman's blossoming pink parts, and she's right. No matter how preoccupied she was with her own fragile mortality at the time, she had to know when that deposit was made.

"Amen," I say.

"I bet it was all for you, though."

"Also true," I tell her, hoping not to sound too conceited.

"You know, that wasn't just chamber stress. He looked at you. Even after he found out what you were going to do he looked at you."

"I know."

"Isn't that weird?" Sunny asks, genuinely perplexed. "I mean, he had to know there was no chance, right?"

"What is it guys say when they want to get you into bed?—'I'd die for you.' I just made him prove it, and under the circumstances he got all he could reasonably expect out of a relationship like this, too."

"I suppose a tragic love story is still a love story."

"I always take it as a compliment," I say, probably a bit too introspectively, then I purposely brighten my voice and add, "Scared, horny, in love or lust, they're thinking about me at the end."

"Are you sure your husband won't get jealous?" It's facetious, but it does beg the question—is there any more intimate relationship than between executioner and condemned, no matter how brief their encounter, how unequal the exchange, or how unpleasant it is for one party? So maybe his suggested intimacy when he looked at my hips and legs and imagined me yielding to him in some other reality was less than I'd already thrust upon him when I told him exactly what I was going to do to him. And his gaze was something I invited with my movements, if I'm honest, but I showed him his place in my world soon enough. Despite my interest in his interest in my profession I hope he understood he was never anything more than material for it.

"As long as we don't kiss hubby's fine with anything I get up to here," I reply, smiling—and he's literally told me that, but he knows I'll never seriously consider touching a customer in that way—I get way too much satisfaction with the intimacy they're sent here for.

Sunny evaluates the man's erection with an expert eye and passes judgment. "Not an impressive penis, though... pretty disappointing, actually."

"I'm sure he heard that before," I say.

"If he had a girlfriend we did her a favor."

"Trust me, the best he could ever hope to pull would be right here," I say, slapping the ass of the woman in front of him gently and watching its cooling flesh jiggle, "and the thought of him balls deep in that makes me sick. We probably did them both favors." It's cruel. It may not even be true, but it brings a smile, and though it's probably not kind to have fun at their expense they're beyond caring now, and both of them got something out of the deal. Sunny doesn't pull out her camera for just any decorated back or opening bud.

"Have you ever thought what it would be like if it was, like, love at first sight?" she asks.

"He was free to love anyone he wanted," I say, turning his body further, inviting her to observe its soft ordinariness which contrasts so starkly with his nearly angry genitals, "but nobody can demand reciprocation."

"No, I mean if you saw a guy come in for processing and you fell in love with him?"

102

"Philosophers say we kill what we love," I tell her after a beat.

"So you'd do it?"

"Yes."

"Without even giving him a little kiss?"

"Oh, I'd give him something," I say, running my finger all the way around my wedding band to prove to myself it really has no beginning and no end. "I've made plans," I confess.

"Yeah, I think I'd get a little thrill, too," Sunny replies, obliviously. "It's not like there aren't other guys to fall in love with, right?"

"They say we're doomed to it, biological switches turning on and off that add or subtract pain and obsession, and when we hit the right configuration by trial and error we call it love."

Sunny redirects her attention to the oozing discharge on the No Fear woman's back and examines it carefully. "Speaking of—do you think she liked getting it?"

"It doesn't matter," I say.

"Seriously."

"It depends on who she thought it was for."

"Oh, she definitely thought it was for her, a hot gooey award for being the world's most desirable woman, heralding the arrival of her reprieve, and news that she won the lottery," Sunny laughs, raising my spirits and I chuckle in reply.

"She wouldn't be the first to delude herself in the dark," I say.

Sunny turns her attention back to my curious boy, staring unapologetically at his erection. "I bet he would have married you," she says. "You know, if you said you'd take him down and sneak him out, and not just to save his own life."

I frown and hold up my hand pointing to my wedding ring. Besides, she knows as well as I that every phase of every customer's trip through the facility is monitored. Their prisoner chips are automatically scanned on arrival and the conveyor system weighs them. They're scanned again as they enter the chamber, their presence correlated with gas concentrations, chamber time, and heart rate data, and finally each group's individual weights are added and compared to the aggregate weight of the flesh disposed of. There's no cheating the system, and I wouldn't have it any other way, even under difficult circumstances.

"No," Sunny tells me, "I don't mean to actually do it, but wouldn't it have been fun to hear him promise undying love right before you processed him?"

"That's better than any promise," I say with a nod, indicating the woman's slimy back.

Sunny smiles and shrugs.

While it's gratifying to look at the fruit of one's labors, I'm starting to get hungry. I let go of the curious boy, allowing him to settle against No Fear gently, watching with some interest exactly where his engorged glans makes contact before sliding up her back through the viscous mess it's left there, clearing a little vertical trough through the congealing liquid as it moves. I give the long legged lady behind him a cursory inspection. Curiously, she's at close to full bloom, too, and the nipples at the tips of her large natural breasts are in a similar state of readiness. I heft one in my hand, give it a squeeze like a ripe peach, rolling the stiff nipple at its end between my thumb and forefinger. I hope many a lover got to do this when she and they could have appreciated it, but now it's just fatty waste to be disposed of. "Open vat two," I instruct.

The vat lids are large. They're round, about eight feet across, made of the same brushed metal as the chambers, and unlike the chamber doors, which are moved hydraulically for convenience, these are far too heavy to lift manually, but they're not as impressive as the vats themselves, which are in the basement, their lids built flush with the floor we're on for easy loading. And though protected by guard rails, between loads they're kept closed, but not locked, for safety, because the rails only go about halfway around the vat openings to allow clearance for the pivoting lids, and they're only single bars, chest high for me, so it's possible to go under them fairly easily, something I almost did one memorable day when I slipped.

Sunny issues the commands through her tablet and the thick steel door begins to tilt open slowly as its hydraulic actuators whine. When viewed edge on you can see the locking mechanism which makes the chambers' vault type doors look insignificant. Pins as thick as my fist ring it. Holes the size of my fist lie between the pins to accept pins that advance from the vat when the locking mechanism is activated. As the pins from the lid advance into holes in the vat, pins from the vat advance into holes in the lid—a double redundant system with either capable of restraining the incredible pressures they operate at. Were a lid that size to fail it wouldn't just go through the roof ahead of a geyser of hideously dangerous unpleasantness, it's only a slight exaggeration to say it would be a hazard to low flying planes, and no exaggeration to say it would crush anything beneath it when it landed, which would ruin the low profile we're trying to maintain, but I'm sure the bureau has a ready-made cover story for almost any eventuality.

"Load vat two."

Group two advances at Sunny's fingertip command, traveling along a little 'S' bend in the rail as they move, as the vats are more widely spaced than the chambers. Like sacrifices of old they were chosen, stripped, bathed, bound, and delivered up for the ritual, and now the first part of the ceremony is complete, but there are no gods left to accept their flesh, so we had to come up with our own way of completing the rite. When each customer hits the vat's safety rail they bend forward as the carrier moving them along the overhead conveyor hits a lever which causes a pin to retract which releases the harness, and customer suspended therefrom, to gravity's devices, allowing them to tumble head first into the vat one after another. Unconstrained by muscle and shame they fall with the graceless elegance of rag dolls, vanishing from this world forever. The first two or three land with echoing metallic clangs when they hit bottom, the rest land on the growing pile of flesh within with dull thuds. I can't help but feel a certain satisfaction as they tumble, my curious boy next to last. Sometimes the final customer of a group will hang up on the safety rail because there's no one behind them to push them in, so Sunny is right there, and grabs the gangly woman's ankles, lifting them over her head sharply as she bends to make sure she flips in, which she does, her large breasts flopping with even more graceless grace than the others'. Then Sunny closes and seals the vat, its locking mechanism slams into place with so much force I can feel it in my toes though I'm ten feet away, because I really don't like to get too close when those lids are open.

When we inspect group one we find the results are similar to two's with everyone having responded in at least a modestly immodest manner, most more than modestly. The highlight of the group is the pregnant lady, though. Her hair's matted, and her face has a rather strange resigned, but well worked, look. Her nipples have tightened moderately, and she's turned a pleasant pink all over, quite pretty actually, which is nice because when with child they often come out blotchy. Even her sweat sheen is almost perfectly even from head to toe, but isn't so heavy that it runs or drips. I probably should have told her she was glowing instead of big as a house, but that's hindsight. It's such a good result Sunny motions me to turn her so she can snap a pic. "We saving this one?" I ask, tapping the bulging belly when she's done.

"Nope," Sunny tells me, "barrel's full."

"Too bad, if the one inside looks as good it'll be a waste to just dump her in the bath. No small ones we can get rid of?"

"Nothing near the top, I can dig down if you want, but with as tight as they're packed it'll take a while to get 'em out and back in. I don't mind, though. It's kind of like doing a three-D jigsaw puzzle with rubber pieces."

"Nah, it's not that important."

"Want me to get the scissors and a towel?" Sunny asks, "just for kicks?"

We start with a fifty-five gallon drum about a third full of brine and harvest customers' fetuses post processing, throwing them in until it's full. To be fair, they never filled fast. Pregnant customers still make up less than one percent of our clientele, and we do pack those barrels pretty tight. With their bones undeveloped their little bodies compress nicely, and when we're finished, like old tins of sardines, there's a lot more flesh than fluid and we often need a mallet to get the lid on. At one time the bureau used to come out and switch barrels as soon as we got one sealed. Now it can be weeks before they send the truck out to collect it and give us a new one. A couple of times they've had us just dump it into a vat on top of a group of customers to get rid of them, which seems like a waste after going to so much trouble to collect them, but what do you do with eighty or more pickled fetuses in varying stages of development from fishy looking things the size of your thumb to babyish looking things the size of an infant if nobody wants them? Supply has simply outpaced demand, even with high schools now using them for dissection in biology classes instead of fetal pigs.

One day, when our barrel was nearly full, I watched a then relatively new apprentice, a diligent, but slightly introspective young man, take three or four slightly smaller than fist sized examples from the brine so he could get a larger one in—standard practice because the bigger they are the greater the value to scientists and scholars. Those removed were right at that stage where they start to look like those weird little twentieth century celluloid carnival dolls, but instead of chucking them into one of the vats like I taught him when we couldn't squeeze more into the barrel with a little creative rearrangement or a lot of compression, he slipped them into a plastic bag and then into his pocket.

"What are you doing?" I asked, more out of curiosity than anything else. I figured either he was engaging in his own anatomical research, or maybe even some kind of art project because he was incredibly creative.

He pulled the bag out and held them up for me. "I hope you don't mind. I've been taking the extras for a while now," he said.

"No, it's fine, as long as you don't tell anyone where they came from, but why are you taking them?"

"They're the perfect snack size," he told me.

I try not to judge people. My whole profession is literally about not passing judgment on my customers, treating every one of them equally, but I'm afraid there was a fair amount of disbelief in my voice when I said, "You're eating them?"

"Oh, my God, no," he replied, unveiled disgust in his voice. "They're for Cain. They're his favorite training treat—just the right size, one mouthful and they're gone so he isn't distracted and we can get back to work."

Cain was his Rottweiler, and held several records in large dog agility competitions. I'm afraid that as soon as he said that the dynamite went off. I totally lost my shit with him, because the thought of those big headed, little limbed, rubbery flesh balls vanishing down Cain's eager gullet with a hollow sounding snap of his jaws followed by an appreciative puppy bark and wagging tail was too much for me. It's the only time I can remember getting really angry at work, but I couldn't believe he was doing that, that he'd be so irresponsible. I mean, it was just unthinkable. I read him the riot act forward and backward. Pickled foods are so bad for dogs, and I couldn't believe he'd risk Cain's health just to get him to go through the weave poles a second faster, and it's not like he didn't love his great big fur baby. That dog was his life. He had, 'Cain,' tattooed on his forearm in huge block letters. He just wasn't thinking, but you have certain responsibilities if you're going to be a pet owner. To his credit he was always quite careful to correctly dispose of excess fetuses after

110

that, and though he wasn't a very sporty type he could get them in a vat from across the room using its lid as a backboard for 'three pointers' as he called them, which probably isn't that difficult when you've got a three inch 'ball' and an eight foot 'basket,' but at least they were going into the right giant maw, one that would never get indigestion. And I did buy a big jar of pig ears for Cain as a way of apologizing for taking away his favorite treat—dried pig ears, not pickled.

We're still called on to bring out the mobile unit every two or three weeks. It's a processing center on wheels built into a motor home, and probably the best part of the reforms has been the near elimination of organ shortages for patients who need transplants. In fact, the system is so good it automatically puts holds on any condemned prisoner who has rare genetics to keep them ready for future need. The occasional stories you hear about prisoners lingering for months, sometimes years, after sentencing is never because they made friends with the right guard, or their families found the right palm to grease, or because of computer errors. They were just unknowingly waiting for the day when their heart, lungs, livers, or other organs would be needed.

On mobile days we go to the detention centers and collect donor customers, no more than six at a time because that's all the storage we have. Then we drive them to the hospital where the patients they've matched with are prepped and ready for surgery, and process their organ donors on the spot, usually in the employee parking lot. It's more than a little cramped inside, but we make the best of it. The spaces are smaller than they need to be because, by protocol, the medical staff there to harvest the organs can't see the customers before processing, so the space is divided. It seems silly because the unit exists to make sure they get nice, fresh, healthy organs ready for transplant, and do they think it's a coincidence we can always deliver donors who are still warm and glassy eyed? When they're ready they tell us which two 'cadavers' they want first via intercom. The mobile chamber is so small that the customers find it even cozier inside than at a normal processing center, but we always manage to get them in it and get it sealed. Its load door is on the 'detention' side that the hospital personnel never see, and its disposal door opens onto the 'morgue' side, a small room with two dissection tables to remove the desired organs, after which they put the spent donors on waste racks and call for the next two cadavers which are ready for them in less than ten minutes. When they're done harvesting, plausible deniability intact, though I do wonder how they'd explain the sounds coming from the other side of that door before the cadavers magically appear if anyone asks, we take the donors back to our center and dispose of them normally.

Sunny's offer is tempting, even if just to take a peek at what's inside that perfectly pink bulging belly out of curiosity, and it would only take a couple of minutes, but we're overdo for a break. "Nah," I tell her, "I don't want one of those, dead or alive, do you?"

She shakes her head.

"Then load vat one." And Sunny soon has group one gliding down their rail towards its dark loading door. Because of her lower center of gravity the mother that was to be does a three quarter flip instead of a half flip as she tumbles in with the same fearless lack of self-consciousness as the others. When the rest have followed her I have Sunny close and lock it, then start both vats' automatic cycles. We wait for the automatic checks to complete, and when she confirms there are no error codes I tell her, "Good job," as the disposal fluid rushes noisily in and the pre-heat begins.

"Lunch?" Sunny asks.

"Lunch," I repeat, "my treat." I take her to a noodle house just down the street. We don't rush. It takes the vats over an hour to go through their cycles, and we're not expecting today's last batch of customers until late afternoon.

When we return, bellies full of ramen, we go down into the basement and look up at the facility's two high pressure disposal vats. Made of the same polished steel as the gas chambers they're even more imposing because most of their plumbing is on the outside, and they're designed to operate under much higher pressure, so all pipes, valves, and doors are heavily reinforced. They are, essentially, raised stainless steel tubes roughly sixteen feet high and eight across, mounted vertically, supported on four thick, spreading legs, with the bottom few feet tapering to a funnel shape that ends with a small unloading door at about shoulder height at the very bottom. Inside each vat there's a cage around six feet in diameter running top to bottom, which keeps the material centered, away from the fluid jets that ring the tank every vertical foot or so, angled to create a whirlpool effect that keeps it moving and exposed to the liquid therein. There's also a winding coil of heat exchange tubing between the cage and outer wall that might otherwise snare loose pieces of the material.

The vats are filled from four tanks that flank them, each much larger than they are, taking up much of the basement space. These hold the premixed disposal solution. Like the vats they're also gleaming metal, cylindrical, standing on end. They're connected to them via a complex plumbing system with automatic valves that ensure any tank can fill either vat, and that any tank can fill any other tank, which simplifies their refilling, which is done at night by tanker trucks from an alley behind the facility two or three times a week, depending on how busy we are.

The vats sound a bit like overgrown dishwashers in operation, and we can tell they're almost finished with their cycles because the pumps have gotten louder to push the thickening fluid through their jets.

The disposal system is alkaline hydrolysis. Everyone knows you can dissolve organic matter in acid. That's how your stomach works—put food in, noodles in our case, and its acid turns it to liquid that your intestines can extract nutrients from. Less known is that the same thing happens if you go the other way on the pH scale.

Highly alkaline solutions are just as destructive to organic tissues as powerful acids, dissolves them just as efficiently, just as completely, but they're much easier to work with. Unlike acids, which aggressively burn through most industrial metals, even the strongest alkaline solutions, called bases, are harmless to them. This means that the pressure vessels, plumbing, and pumps can all be made of standard industrial grade stainless steel, which makes design and construction easy, cost and maintenance minimal, and rollout fast. They are, essentially, gigantic robotic stomachs that operate at the other end of the pH scale digesting the customers within, reducing them to liquid almost completely by immersing them in a solution chemically similar to the strongest drain cleaners.

It's a process that was developed to turn slaughter house sweepings into fertilizer in the eighteen hundreds. A hundred and fifty years later it was adapted to dispose of dead indigents and people who donated their bodies to medical schools because it's cheaper than cremation, which came in after the second world war as an easier alternative to potter's field burials when states and municipalities saw how efficient the Nazis were at using fire to get rid of their unwanted populace. Why symbolically return someone to the earth when it's such a bother to dig a hole, let alone erect a small marker of remembrance for a life lived?

Then, with the global warming scare, entrepreneurs started selling hydrolysis as a 'green' way of disposing of people's loved ones by calling it 'water cremation,' because the more accurate 'chemical liquefaction,' and 'corrosive dissolving,' are less palatable to potential clients, and it's hard enough to convince anyone to turn their departed kin to sewage, so a little clever wordplay was needed, and profitable. And even when people learn the actual term they hear 'hydro' and think 'water.' Water is clean, life giving, natural, and when pregnant customers hear about hydro baths for their babies they relax, imagining a very different kind of water birth than they'll actually get. Though benign sounding, hydrolysis is actually a blanket term for a chemical reaction that tears organic compounds into their component parts with the aid of a water molecule's electrons. The closer you get to either end of the pH scale the more energetic this reaction. If you liquefy flesh in acid it's acid hydrolysis. If you liquefy it in a base it's alkaline hydrolysis. It doesn't make any difference to the flesh which reaction is turning it to goo—it's still goo in the end.

Each of our vats is large enough to dissolve a chamber full of customers simultaneously. And like the systems we adapted from the cattle and funeral industries before us the highly caustic liquid is whirled with high pressure fluid jets, agitated by ultrasound, and heated to over a hundred fifty degrees centigrade to make the solution more chemically reactive and help break down tissues faster. They're pressurized to north of five hundred kPa, which keeps the superheated liquid from boiling and drives it deep into bodily openings, filling customers' lungs and sinuses almost instantly, eroding the least dense things it encounters first, so the fluid pops the eyes and breaks the thin bones behind them to gain quick access to the brain as it rapidly forces its way into the circulatory system of the torso below, digesting blood and bile as the gas released by the process bursts arteries, veins, and capillaries; dissolving from the inside as well as out accelerates the whole process.

The cowhide harnesses aren't fully tanned, and are manufactured to be porous, perforated with dozens of nearly microscopic holes per square centimeter so the solution penetrates and dissolves them quickly, freeing their prisoners as their bodies begin to break down, skin sloughing off and dissolving, followed by testicles, which are only attached by thin spermatic cords that melt away quickly, then slabs of bubbling body fat and breasts detach. Intestines, stomachs, livers, and other organs in the abdominopelvic cavities, as well as the fetuses of pregnant customers, then float away fizzing into the swirling solution, and when no longer contained by their weakening diaphragms, melting hearts and lungs flow out of rib cages, and muscles loosen and detach, leaving customers' articulated skeletons to swim naked in the swirling soup of mixed organs topped by skulls trailing slicks of dissolving brain seeping through their eye sockets and spinal openings.

Bony arms and legs flail in the dark under the influence of the fluid's motion helping to tear the melting tissues into smaller pieces, exposing ever more

117

surface area for the solution to eat away, until finally tendons, ligaments, and cartilage swell, soften and fail, and the skeletons fall to pieces as the hungry solution eats into the bones themselves, stripping away most of their minerals, weakening them until they begin to break and erode as they rub or pass close to high pressure circulation jets. Organs become unidentifiable as they jelly then dissolve into a well mixed slurry, which itself dissolves into a satisfyingly homogeneous effluent the consistency and color of maple syrup, though skewing a touch more toward green than gold. And since internal sensors in the system automatically balance the amount of alkaline solution with the mass of organic material to be consumed, when the vat's cycle is complete its pH has fallen to a level that's safe to flush into the sewer system.

The process is so amazingly complete that not only does not a single cell remain undigested, but not a single molecule of DNA does, either—even those inside bone and teeth; all remains are rendered biologically inert, ensuring no possibility of a bio-engineered clone resurrection for anyone who ends up in that solution, and though this may seem a tad blasphemous, what we do is so thorough that if there is a God even she would find it so much trouble to reverse our efforts that it's safe to assume she wouldn't bother with holy resurrection, either. When we're done with them they're gone forever, but that's the intent.

The vats are almost finished with our current customers. The high pressure pumps stop within a few minutes of each other, and low pressure pumps begin cooling the settling fluid through the built in heat exchangers that spiral around their interior walls in the form of a single helix. A short time later when the liquid cools to the point that it won't flash boil at atmospheric pressure valves open and vent the containers with long gentle sighs of contentment that release a sweet, slightly earthy aroma, not altogether unpleasant, as green LEDs illuminate on the vats' monitoring systems, first on two, then one, indicating that it's safe to empty them.

"Drain vat two," I tell Sunny. She taps her tablet a few times, and as the automatic valves open the viewport in the discharge pipe turns a dark greenish brown as the hot liquid containing its customers' every love, every dream, every hope, every fear, and every memory is drained through it and into the sewer. They all probably imagined they were more than this. I have to admit I take more pleasure than I should in proving them wrong. I only wish my curious boy could see himself flowing away with the others, part of a single, syrupy amalgam, but I give him a sly smile and little rippling finger wave when Sunny isn't looking and whisper, "You're welcome," to him, and I mean it.

I'm sure he would have preferred a different disposal method, but when the shock wore off he would have been impressed by how quickly and efficiently he and his fellow travelers were reduced to something so easily disposed of. But I'm not sorry I misled him when he asked about being dissolved in acid. I didn't lie, though.

119

A caustic alkaline solution is, quite truthfully, the furthest thing you can get from an acid. I just didn't volunteer that it has the same effect on bodily tissues and would be used to dispose of him and everyone else processed here, because that's all he was; that's all any of them were by the time they showed up—sentient sewage. If he'd asked the necessary followup questions I would have told him; I'm proud of what we do, but he didn't, because despite his curiosity I don't think he wanted to know that this was all ready and waiting for him. When I offered an off-ramp he took it, and eagerly. If he hadn't he probably would have fixated on the disposal and not the processing, and the processing was the last thing he could experience, ever, and I didn't want to take that from him by filling him with anxiety about things he'd never witness, never feel.

I knew, and that was enough.

After a few minutes the gurgling in the vat tells us that it's almost empty, a final rhythmic threnody for liquefied humanity seeking its level. It's no surprise that it always seems to be lower, and it's not like anyone would want to build monuments to these losers anyway—and I don't mean that as a pejorative. It's merely descriptive, not judgmental. From the moment customers arrive until the moment they're drained away I'm actually quite protective of them, but whatever game is played to determine who is and who isn't, who condemns people to conversion to liquid, and who becomes that liquid, regardless of the rules or whether they're fair, these people have lost. Perhaps the best way to describe my feelings towards them is they're like lovers you bed out of pity. You don't fuck them because you hate them, but when it's over it's actually kinder to make sure they know you're done with them, so you send them on the walk of shame, but it's not out of spite, and disposal is, in a way, the ultimate walk of shame—no, I won't be calling you tomorrow. As the last of the effluent passes by the view port it leaves just a few brownish drops clinging to the inside of the glass.

And this is the part that makes it difficult to find good assistants. I don't understand the squeamishness some people have about the method. After processing, the customers, regardless of what they were before, are just carcasses, but unlike cattle, poultry, and pigs, which don't acquire their actual value until after slaughter, when our chamber doors open all that comes out is waste flesh that must be disposed of, a ton and a half of it every time. At the rate we're processing it's not just that other methods are inferior, they're infeasible. For a while converting it to animal feed was something the reformers pursued with zealot-like enthusiasm. Not wasting a resource appealed to their twin philosophies of economics and ecology, and technology seemingly put that dream within reach. Most large scale animal butchering is done by machine these days. The same industrial robots that can assemble a car can disassemble an animal if you replace automatic wrenches and welding equipment with saws, knives, and claws, and with the same speed and precision—as long as you give them splash protection.

Modifying a line designed for porcine anatomy only required a few sensor changes and software updates. Back when we were still cremating I got a chance to see the pilot animal feed plant in operation, was able to spend two or three days a week there for a couple of months learning and helping to improve the system. The chambers were similar, but customers would be processed inverted, suspended by their ankles. After leaving it a knife equipped robotic arm would quickly put two slits in each of their throats severing their jugular veins for bleeding, and after exsanguination large rotary saws removed heads and limbs in just fractions of a second, sending each down their separate disassembly lines as the torsos proceeded down theirs. Torches on each would dehair and bubble the skin to loosen it, and after a few cuts with automatic knives it could be peeled off like tight stockings, opera gloves, leotards, and ski masks, with a myriad of appropriately sized and spaced hooks on wringer-like pinch wheels.

I found the torso line to be most interesting. There were a number of stations, each with two robotic arms, one for cutting, one for grabbing. The torsos would stop for two or three seconds at each one. Slabs of fat were sliced away first, followed by pectoral and oblique and other abdominal muscles, and customers selected for this program were kept in detention for two extra months with a more carefully controlled diet for a bit of fattening up to make sure they had the desired muscle, organ, fat ratio. Next the torsos would be eviscerated one organ at a time. Livers, intestines, stomachs, etc. were plucked and dropped into their cooling bins first, but what was truly impressive was that the arms had the articulation and dexterity to reach into rib cages and pluck lungs and hearts, the lungs always coming away as a pair still neatly joined by their windpipes, and it all happened at lightning speed, with every organ cut free from adjoining organs, connective tissue, and the vascular system without putting a nick on them. I hate to say it, but these robots could put any human butcher to shame—if there's a John Henry with a butcher's knife out there, a Jack the Ripper for the modern age, he's a walking dead man if he ever tries his luck against these bots.

On a parallel line a machine would wrench *mandibles* off the heads hydraulically so tongues could be easily sliced out, then their eyes were rapidly removed with a suction device, one at a time, and their sockets drilled through with hole saws, after which a blast of high pressure air through the *foramen magnum* would jelly the brain and blow it out through the eye sockets against a splash guard so the material would slide down into a collection bin that would fill with something that looked like a yellowish gray chunky custard streaked with red, and while it wasn't terribly pleasant to look at, it was better than the bin with the eyes because there was something unsettling about seeing the occasional blue eye peeking out from all the brown, and when I talked to the other employees I wasn't alone in that, so I tested it by hand sorting blue and brown eyes into different buckets, and the others agreed that it was less disturbing even when the buckets were side by side, so, for the comfort of the staff I suggested that when full scale plants were built eyes should be segregated by color, either with separate vacuum plucking machines for each, or some kind of automatic sorting device similar to those that separate red from green tomatoes at harvest. In the end a junior engineer on the project came up with a much simpler solution, dropping the eyes into a spinning blade device immediately after plucking and collecting the resultant pulp instead of the eyes themselves, which would only be pulped later anyway.

The final line would cut muscles from the skinned arms and legs, with the robots' optical and AI system able to adjust for either, even when presented at random, and the contractor assured us they could handle any size we could present them, from those of the tallest man to those from the shortest dwarf, all automatically, and without the need for adjustment or hand sorting. At the end the three lines would converge and the mostly de-fleshed bones would be fed into a crushing machine with slow turning opposing intermeshing gears the diameter and width of asphalt-roller wheels, shattering them to extract their marrow. I have to admit it took a while to get used to the sights and sounds of it at work—articulated bloody boned arms and legs flailing as it pulled them in, the machine gun like cracks and pops of rib cages and spines as they were splintered, or the way hollow skulls would just fold up with hardly a cracker crunch as they slowly vanished between the glistening red teeth, especially if their eye sockets were facing out as they were ingested, but you get used to anything, and in time I learned to marvel at how efficiently the machine did its job, and I could even laugh when a fleshy skeletal hand would look like it was waving bye-bye if the gears grabbed the shoulder end of a *humerus* just right and shook the arm as it pulled it in, before the hand, too, vanished slowly with its accompanying bubble wrap popping sound.

The system was amazing, both in scope and detail, and while the robots' dexterity was impressive it's their speed that made them truly awe inspiring. From the time they took charge of a customer until their marrow was extracted was just a few minutes, and they didn't operate sequentially. Multiple customers were on the lines simultaneously, stopping for a few seconds in front of each robot then moving forward in perfect synchronization when each had performed its assigned task until there was nothing left. It really was like watching an assembly line in reverse, if more biological in nature. I even asked the manager if we could run the line backward once. He didn't get the joke and replied, "Who the hell would want to?"

It was just a pilot program, though, and only disposed of a hundred or so customers a week, usually all on the same day so durability and throughput could be evaluated in real world conditions. Other days were used for tweaking the machinery. Sometimes a few customers were brought in and run through one at a time to test changes and make adjustments, and I'm afraid it could be a long day for them as they waited for the technicians to finish their mods then call for the next one, and I always felt bad sending them into the chamber one at a time, because that's not a place you want to be alone, but it was to help speed things up for those who would follow *en masse*, so the needs of the individual had to be subjugated to those of the group. I don't think I'll ever forget how pathetic one person screaming into the blackness can be, though. I'd want to tell them, 'I know you think it's unfair, but we've decided you're going now, so just take a few nice deep breaths for me,' and eventually they did, or they yelled themselves out like a tired toddler, and a few minutes later we'd have the material for the technicians to get on with their work.

The final step was to take the separated components and reintegrate them on demand in the correct proportions. Farmers enrolled in the program would order feed with the nutrient balance and pellet size appropriate for their livestock. I seem to recall pigs requiring a higher percentage of brain and cattle more lung, but whatever was ordered, the system would weigh and mix the appropriate ingredients, pulp it, blend it with a cornmeal base, then extrude the pellets, dry and package the finished product, and send it out. They raved about the quality and price of the feed the system produced, and were eager to order in volume. Of course, they didn't know what kind of animal was supplying the supplements they ordered, but it doesn't really matter as mammalian organs are remarkably similar in composition from species to species, so it's pretty much the same if the pig supplying the bacon you're eating has gotten its iron from the livers of its brethren, from those of the cows whose milk you're putting in your coffee, or from those of people with unpopular positions on social issues. When it comes right down to it meat is meat, so why be prudish about where it comes from?

Those were pretty heady times. I mean, it all just worked, and I really thought I was looking at the future of disposal. I actually got pretty excited about the idea of recycling spent customers into something useful. I even volunteered to work at the first full scale plant. Unfortunately, the program was canceled after its proof of concept period ended, because as impressive as it was, it wasn't without issues. Not only were there concerns over contagion risk if you put that much human flesh in the food supply, even indirectly—think of the potential for Mad Cow or some other prion disease on a much larger scale, which would lead to investigations and the other major issue, plausible deniability. While automation would alleviate the need for a large trustworthy workforce handling knives and doing the cutting, this led to concerns about the amount of maintenance required for all that machinery, which would include the need to have a fair number of technicians performing calibration and testing on the species of animal being butchered, and could lead to potentially embarrassing exposure. One leaked video of customers' skinned torsos having their livers plucked at the rate of one every few seconds punctuated by that weird slippery 'shlurp' sound they made when they were dropped into their bin had the potential to turn public opinion faster than a drill sergeant on parade. There was an easy way to prevent that, but it's never pleasant to have to cull staff to keep secrets, so something more suitable had to be devised.

Burial was out of the question—takes far too much time, far too much ground, hallowed or not, and there's no chance the powers that be would agree to any disposal method that might leave something behind because unmarked mass graves, while simple, can invite judgment on those who created them, even if not discovered until decades later, but that's not really the point. While customers pay for their misdeeds and misthoughts with their lives, when they're removed from their chamber the job is only half done; the culture isn't truly cleansed until every part of them has vanished forever, until all that's left of them is an unpleasant memory that fades as quickly as new undesirables are discovered.

And cremation, which served well during the initial phases of the reforms, and I have nothing against it—I trained at a burn facility—has issues, too. A properly designed system, with continuous-feed ovens and automatic bone grinding, is about as convenient as it can get for the operators. After processing, you drop the customers into the feed hopper, fire up the system, then empty the ash hopper into a waiting dumpster when its cycle is complete, and it's away to the landfill when the dumpster's full. Sounds ideal, but nobody really liked cremation. From the bureau's perspective the problem was cost. When you scale up ovens for the throughput we need they get big and expensive and consume enormous quantities of energy that can't be used for other purposes, regardless of whether it's gas from the ground for traditional incineration, or electricity from solar and wind farms for a greener alternative. And for the crews it was hot, sweaty work, even in winter, and no matter how careful you were, you were always sooty by the end of the day. It would just get everywhere, really, and you'd go home smelling it, tasting it, needing a shower, and having to send your clothes to the dry cleaner.

I can't tell you how thrilled I was the first time I saw hydrolysis disposal in action. It was more exciting than even the animal feed solution because it was so much simpler. It was a godsend being able to just melt all that surplus flesh and watch it flow down the drain with no chance of anyone seeing what happened inside those miracle vats as they worked, but I've had three trainees for whom it was a deal breaker. They didn't have the slightest problem watching customers shuttled into the chambers knowing what was about to happen to them, or with the sounds emanating from them during processing, or seeing the lifeless bodies slide out when it was over, but they blanched at the sight of their liquefied remains running by the discharge pipe's little window. One ran out retching a few seconds after it began. I thought he had potential and tried to talk him back, told him the effluent was the byproduct of a job well done and something to take pride in, that he'd get used to it, that we're all made of the same stuff so if we were in the vats and somebody else was doing the disposal we'd look just like that, but I couldn't entice him to empty that second vat and had to let him go— told him he wasn't cut out for the work and wished him well. Two others stuck it out through the first drainings, through the next processings, but one couldn't bring himself to push the button to load the vats again. The other managed that, but had a complete breakdown when she started the cycle and heard the hydrolysis solution pouring in. She actually ran to the vat lid crying and tried to pry it open with her fingernails.

I had to call her mother to come get her.

And though sworn to secrecy, all three, and the mother, ended up back for processing within a week of their failings, were probably arrested the same day I reported the circumstances of their departures, something I had to do if I didn't want to risk ending up in one of those vats myself, but it did leave me the sad job of reducing them to what disgusted them so much, and it really was a shame about the mom. They didn't make it difficult for me, though, so either they understood or were in shock, and though I always work quickly to mitigate anxiety I was extremely diligent with their groups. I mean, you can't really blame them for not being able to hack it, but the powers that be are understandably concerned that the public, which is extremely supportive of certain groups vanishing as long as they don't know the details, might react badly to learning that they're being reduced to brown syrupy goo and flushed into the sewers, no matter how cost effective it is for the taxpayers and green it is for the environment, and so go to great lengths to make sure no one who isn't one hundred percent reliable is able to blow a whistle.

Luckily, I finally found Sunny who's just as enthusiastic about this part of the job as every other. I have her activate the flush system which rinses vat two with fresh water for several minutes until it runs crystal clear. Group one is then drained and their vat and discharge pipe is, likewise, rinsed clean. "Baby out with the bathwater," Sunny tells me when it's done.

"Empty vat two," I order, trying to keep a straight face, and Sunny triggers the automatic system that unlocks and partially opens and vibrates its bottom door while simultaneously starting the fine mesh metal conveyor belt that crawls beneath it at waist height. The only material in a corpse that alkaline hydrolysis can't liquefy is calcium phosphate, so all that's left to empty are the dripping bones and teeth of our customers, or more precisely, what appear to be their bones and teeth. They're a bit like the skeletons of skeletons. With all other minerals stripped away they're so porous you can crush them in your hands, and if you find one that appears unbroken and snap it in two you'll find it hollow, the marrow or pulp completely dissolved and washed away with the other organic material through the pores the solution has etched through them, which is incredibly invasive and aggressive, especially in the high pressure and heat of an operating hydrolysis system. What's left is the consistency of a medium chalk and white as snow, and yes, you can even write with it on a rough enough surface. One of my assistants, whom I dubbed Caravaggio, quite good, but not with me very long, was an accomplished artist who would sometimes create elaborate works in the parking lot with it on his lunch break, using *femurs* for broad strokes, *ulnas* for fine, and sections of skull for fill. He even made quite a good portrait of me once as a peace offering—he was the one I blew my top at when I caught him using excess pickled fetuses as dog treats, so he made a full body rendering of me kneeling and hugging Cain, whom he rendered with a big bone in his mouth. It was so good it was a shame to see it fade away through wear and weather, but parking lot art is ephemeral by nature, as we are, I guess. I have a picture of it somewhere, though, and it might even outlast me, if the cloud it's stored in does.

Most of the material dropping onto the conveyor belt has already been severely eroded or broken to small pieces by the tank's circulation jets and ultrasound, and is unrecognizable as anything other than debris, giving it a rather pretty confetti-esque look that glints in the light as it tumbles down wet with rinse water. Naughty as it may be, this is what I was picturing in my mind's eye as I stared at the side of my curious boy's head while we talked, as I examined the tiny pinprick beads

132

of perspiration on the side of his brow, wondering whether any identifiable part of his skeleton would remain after the vat had its way with him, its calcium shard remnants proving I don't need acid to do my job more completely than he could ever have imagined in that soon to be liquefied brain of his. Since he was to be one of the last into the vat, and therefore near the top, his remains would be more thoroughly pulverized than those lower down, because like a raging ocean the churning currents are strongest near the surface, but the cascade is just starting and this is where the occasional larger pieces tend to be.

If you know what to look for you'll see relatively whole pelvic bones like *sacra* and *ilia* falling, but almost never a whole pelvis because they tend to be levered apart as they mix. A handful of long bones, mostly femurs, and a couple of skulls, sans jaws, drop onto the conveyor belt relatively intact. The latter is a bit unusual. Whole, or nearly whole skulls, even those wrenched off of customers lowest in the vats relatively early in their cycles, are the unicorns of disposal. It's rare to get one, and even if they survive the chemicals, heat, and mixing, they become so fragile I've seen them break just dropping onto the mesh conveyor belt. So two surviving, while not unheard of, happens maybe once every hundred disposals. My first long term assistant enjoyed finding those. He'd punch them and laugh himself silly when his fist went through them, imagining he could hit someone so hard he could push their face out of the back of their head, or he'd dropkick them to see how widely he could scatter the shattering pieces, and though I do like to maintain a level of professionalism and decorum, it really is just waste at this point, and it's important to have a fun workplace, so I let him amuse himself as he learned the trade as long as he cleaned up the mess, and he liked it when I called him Skull Crusher.

He runs a processing center up north now. When he was promoted I gave him a twenty-five jewel skeleton watch to celebrate. He still sends me a Christmas card every year. It usually has a skeleton on it. I have no idea where he gets them.

The material sounds something like broken crockery falling into sand as it lands on the taut metal mesh conveyor belt. In two or three minutes what's left of group two has been deposited along about twenty feet of it leaving the remains in pretty much a single layer. When the system detects that the vat is empty it stops automatically. This is a much more manageable solid waste situation. There's only about a hundred pounds of material left to dispose of, roughly five per customer. For the first year or so after we started hydrolysis we'd just landfill it—it was so frangible that after compacting there wouldn't be anything identifiable left, and the pea gravel sized pieces would break down in just months, which gave someone a great idea on how to put it to better use, so now there's one more step in the processing, but first we have to walk the length of the belt looking for artificial joints. The detention center medical departments are supposed to let us know if any of the customers have them, and though most are far too young for hip or knee replacements it never hurts to double check.

I processed a famous gymnast, retired, and though she was only in her forties she came with a large print memo pinned to her harness warning that she had two hip replacements. Since those memos are designed to attract attention it's impossible to hide them from the customers so labeled, so detention center personnel are told to tell the customers they're to let us know about their health issues and potential special needs when they attach them, not that they're to warn us to look for metal parts in their crumbling skeletal remains a couple of hours hence. The gymnast, though, was still an amazing physical specimen. More than twenty years after her last competition her legs were still impressively toned, short, obviously, like most gymnasts', but so toned. I'm glad she was retired because it would have been a shame to cut a storied career like hers short. I remember watching her in some championship meet on TV when I was a kid; she did this vault where she just seemed to soar impossibly into the air twisting and flipping at the same time then stuck the landing with this whack that echoed through the auditorium, and I was just thinking—how? How does she do that? It was so inspiring. And unlike a lot of celebrities she didn't seem to think she deserved any kind of special treatment when she showed up for processing—not that most actually ask for it. They never say, 'Do you know who I am?,' or anything like that, but when they realize they've been recognized you can see the expectation, then the surprise when they're shuttled into the chamber with their group, but she just stared straight ahead the whole time, right between the shoulder blades of a man who must have been a foot taller than she, jaw clenched, slightly pale like many customers when they realize it's the beginning of the end.

I did take note of the way she went into the disposal vat after, but the magic was gone. She flipped into it exactly like all the others, and there was no whack of a stuck landing, just a thud when she hit the pile, and more thuds as others landed on top of her. And sure enough when the disposal cycle was complete and the vat emptied we found two beautifully crafted titanium prostheses on the conveyor belt amidst the bone debris. They're in my curio cabinet at home, one on top of the other, their long stems crossing at an acute angle, mirrored heads several inches apart. Most people think they're a pop art sculpture when they first see them. Then I tell them to take a closer look, and they're like, 'Wow.' They even have tiny little etched serial numbers on them so I can prove they were really hers if I ever decide to sell, though I won't be able to say exactly how I acquired them.

Fillings from teeth are too small to worry about, and soft enough for the next stage. Near the vat end of the conveyor belt Sunny points to something and smiles; a twinkling blue eye stares up at us blankly from between some bone fragments. Well, it's not an eye, but a contact lens unscathed by the hydrolysis solution. The detention centers are supposed to confiscate them as soon as prisoners are taken into custody, but sometimes they don't notice. Sunny reaches into the debris and pulls it out. "Wow," she says, "that's pretty."

"It was the tattooed lady's," I tell her. I'd noticed how blue her eyes were when I gave the customers the once over on arrival, and suspected they were too good to be true, but it would have been a bitch move to reach up, hold each eye open, and pry them out one by one, especially in front of the others. It would have looked like an admonition, and if she got that far with them there was no reason not to let her think she was getting away with something, and besides, they were destined for the garbage either way.

Sunny touches the back of the lens with the tip of her tongue then presses it against her forehead hard enough to get it to stick. "Boss, what do you think, enlightenment?"

"Hardly."

"Yeah, not my style," she tells me, picking it off and flicking it onto the floor. "Want me to find the other one?" she asks, already rooting through the fragments in that area.

"No, it's just plastic."

"Right," she replies, and reaches up to open the vat's bottom door all the way manually before reaching inside and pulling the *vertebrae*, *patellas*, teeth, and multiple handfuls of bone fragments that always get deposited around the door's lip and drops them onto the conveyor belt. These are things I don't want to do dressed as I am. I like to appear nice for the customers. I make an effort for them, always have my hair, lipstick, and nails done and flawless. It's a way to both show and command respect, and what Sunny's doing is a somewhat wet endeavor, and I don't like to get dripped on, especially my face and bare toes. Next she checks the ring of strong magnets the material fell through. All the prisoner chips and heart rate monitors are made with ferrous metal inserts so they stick to it. All the HRMs are there, but one of the prisoner chips, which are fairly small, about the size of a cat's or dog's, is missing. It probably wouldn't jam the machinery, but Sunny, ever the perfectionist, carefully reaches into the vat again and feels around the door's lip. She manages to pull out a few more bone fragments, but not finding the chip she looks in the next most likely place, shaking the intact skulls. Those that survive tend to have fallen off early in the disposal from customers low in the vat. They usually land upside down so they collect things that settle after them. They both rattle. The first contains only bone chips and a couple of teeth, but when she looks in the second she sees what she's looking for, and with a few experienced little tilts she gets the wayward chip to fall through the *foramen magnum* into her waiting hand, then tosses it into the magnetic field so it clicks against the closest magnet.

"That's all of them," she tells me, replacing the fragile artifact back on the conveyor belt with care.

I smile. Beginning to end she has such rapport with

the customers. When she became my apprentice I went on a few trips to collect them with her, and the first time she encountered one reluctant to go she pulled out the animal prod without hesitation exactly as she was supposed to, which is good because sometimes noobs hesitate to show them who's boss and give the necessary incentive. They don't have a choice. They're getting on the bus. They're going to be suspended, and now. But instead of administering the shock to get him moving she held it up, explained what it was, and calmly offered him the choice of moving with it or without it. I didn't think it would work. By the time they balk they're usually beyond reason, but there was something in the tone of her voice, so warm, so friendly, that it got through to him, and he went with her like a little lamb, the electrodes against his skin the whole way to make sure he knew he still had the second option. I had to make sure she would use it if necessary, though, so I ordered her to give him a jolt after she got him suspended, which she did. Without an instant's hesitation she drove the long electrodes through the man's skin and directly into his right *gluteus maximus* all the way to the body of the device and pressed the button, causing a horrific scream and convulsion. She unskewered him like lightning then drove them into his perineum and gave him another jolt without me asking. The poor guy yelped like a dying seal and jumped so hard the strap he was suspended from actually went slack for a moment, making me laugh, but calling my bluff with alacrity. Finally, she placed the electrodes hard against the back of his scrotum, stretching it with their points and smiling, daring me to give her a sign to drive them in, "You wouldn't," I say, giving her a disbelieving little smile.

It wasn't a challenge, nor was it a nod to some kind of old fashioned theory of bodily propriety—both of us knew those testicles would be digested by one of the vats within hours, so their evolutionary function was forfeit, and their damage, or lack thereof, not a concern, but even with their purpose reduced to getting the man they were attached to into one of those vats as easily as possible I didn't think Sunny would skewer them. It was merely an observation based on my perception of my new, happy, apprentice, an observation that was incorrect. She drove the electrodes through his skin so that each one impaled the fleshy part of one of his testicles, and with less effort than I would have thought. They were sharper than they looked.

The man's eyes opened wide, and there was a kind of disbelief on his face when he looked down and saw their metal points protruding from the front of his scrotum. When he realized that the unthinkable had, in fact, happened, he started to whisper, "Please," but stopped when Sunny pushed the prod's button and electrified the instrument, causing him to freeze with barely a vocalization, and though his penis remained quite soft, it began slowly oozing semen within a few seconds.

"That's normal," Sunny observed. "His whole reproductive system is overloaded, but there's no

140

pleasure associated with that discharge," and the empty terrified look in his eyes confirmed he was feeling anything but passion. I should have felt sorry for him, but his reaction was so unexpected I could only observe with interest, and in fairness he was fair game once he balked, so even if he did eventually cooperate he was the right one to test Sunny's resolve and technique on. "And did you notice? He didn't scream. He didn't jump. With all their nerves firing he's feeling something that registers as profoundly unpleasant, but it isn't exactly pain because his brain can't process all the signals at once, but in this state all he wants to do is please in hopes of getting it to stop—watch." She looked the man in the eye and ordered, "Sing for me," as he dripped.

The man gave a rendition of *Twinkle, Twinkle, Little Star* in a soft, breathy, nearly robotic voice. He sang the whole thing, then fell silent, a tormented automaton ready to execute its next order.

"They do whatever you ask," Sunny told me. "It gives them a certain dry eagerness. It's kind of endearing, actually. I mean, I like it when they just cooperate, and I have to give them every chance, but I think I prefer induced cooperation." She released the button and the man fell slack in his harness. I don't think he was unconscious, but he didn't move at all when Sunny slowly withdrew the electrodes, which left only four pinprick marks in his skin, two where the electrodes entered his scrotum, two where they exited, with barely a droplet of blood at each. It was an amazing demonstration, and it had been a long time since an apprentice taught me anything, so I'm glad I kept an open mind. If, however, I'd detected any sadism on Sunny's part we would have had a little talk. In this business it pays to enjoy and take pride in the work, even the outcome, but not to enjoy the actual killing or inflicting pain to get to that outcome—and there is a difference. I did ask about the prod, though. Its electrodes weren't standard. On normal animal prods they aren't sharp enough to break skin for fear of damaging the meat beneath. You don't want to lose a steak or roast just because an animal hesitates to move onto the kill line. It turns out that while she was in the early stages of training, before her apprenticeship, Sunny sought out and got permission from the bureau to modify hers on a trial basis, and that's when I knew I had quite a go-getter on my hands, and it wouldn't surprise me to see her design as the new standard in the not too distant future. One of the things I love about this industry is the constant innovation, the drive to improve things, to do them faster, do them better.

Harness buckles in the conveyor debris were a problem when we opened the facility, with each harness having eight. They don't need that many, but it was found that the more controlled a customer feels the less likely they are to struggle. The psychologists consulted said that numerous snug straps limiting movement don't just serve the practical purpose of restraint, but that they're comforting, makes them feel like they're being hugged and keeps them calm as they're moving through the system, and it seems to be the case. They hang quite passively when being moved, and even when they see the waiting chambers, with heart rates rising significantly only as they're being loaded, and when the lights go out at the start of processing, while struggles only begin in earnest after the gas injection system is activated, but the design is so good that not one customer has ever gotten so much as a single hand free, which would be horrible, not because they might escape; they're locked in a gas tight steel box after all, but because it would be cruel to give them false hope, and we do want this to be as humane as possible. The only thing they should be anticipating once processing starts is the certainty of taking another breath and getting one step closer to unconsciousness, which as a practical matter is the end of their personal journeys. Despite this excellent harness design, when the buckles were steel it would add to our workload. Shielded by the mass of falling bone some would always get through the magnets and play hide and seek among the fragments on the conveyor belt, and with so many there were occasional miscounts and machinery jams—not serious, but annoying nonetheless. Luckily a new buckle design ended that nightmare. They're injection molded, made from wood pulp and bio-degradable glue. They're more than durable enough for the job, as proven every day when highly motivated customers test them like their lives depend on it, yet come out of the chambers as securely restrained as when they went in, but, like the straps, these buckles are completely consumed with the other organic material in the vats.

The only real trouble we ever had with the system was back when the prisoners still showed up wearing their detention jumpsuits under their harnesses. We had many, many processings that went without a hitch—customers in, effluent out, like clockwork, but the time we had a problem it was a doozy. When the facility opened we sent memos to all the detention centers in the area telling them to be certain customers arrived wearing only cotton or some other natural fiber. We couldn't tell them why, because even though the centers know why they're sending prisoners to us the reformers decided the disposal method was so sensitive that only those directly involved should know. But in time whoever was organizing the centers either forgot or became complacent. Then they changed their uniform supplier, and one day a full load of customers showed up in nice new orange synthetic jumpsuits and nobody noticed. I guess we could have checked every time, but honestly, some synthetics look quite natural, and it's hard to look at tags inside clothing when people are wearing them and bound, and besides, those responsible for dressing them had been informed of the acceptable materials for their uniforms. The trouble is that many synthetics are, like metals, invulnerable to strong alkaline solutions, and the system requires the tissues to be constantly exposed to the turbulent disposal liquid to soften then melt them away. It's a bit like putting sugar cubes in your tea. When you stir it, it happens fairly quickly. When you don't, you get blobs of slumped sugar at the bottom of your cup.

The processing was normal, and all seemed well during disposal—until we tried to open the first vat and discharge the solid waste. We were expecting a cascade of white bones and shards as usual. What we got were wads of orange cloth oozing thick yellow brown muck gumming up the opening. Looking more carefully we discovered that all the customers' heads, hands, feet, and about half of each limb had liquefied and flowed away normally, but their torsos and the upper part of each limb, protected by the synthetic cloth, had been soaked in the solution, had absorbed the solution, had reacted with the solution, but very little had dissolved away into it because the wrapped flesh wasn't exposed to the tank's whirling currents, leaving us with twenty gelatinous torsos wrapped in jumpsuits lumped together in a sludgy mess at the bottom of the vat amidst the fragments of their crushed skulls and *phalanges* forming a glutinous plug that prevented anything from coming out. This was before Sunny's time. Luckily Skull Crusher was with me and not some trainee. He seemed to think of it as a challenge, and was perfectly content to take the lead because he knew I didn't like reaching up into the dripping vats, but this happened in my facility on my watch, so I wasn't about to take a back seat no matter how messy the task or how nicely I was dressed, not that he ended up looking any better than me by the time we were finished. I had a heck of a time figuring out how to get those things out of the vat. If I tried to grab a protruding *radius* or *femur* head, though slippery, I could get a pretty good grip on it because of the ball on the end, but if I pulled they'd just pop out with this little suction noise or break and I'd end up holding a slimy bone or piece thereof. If I reached into a warm gooey neck to grab a customer's backbone the *vertebrae* would detach one by one with barely a tug no matter how deep I forced my hand until it was almost like they were taunting me, and I have to admit to throwing one in frustration when it became obvious this technique wouldn't work, either. It hit one of the half empty disposal solution tanks with a hollow ring that reverberated through the otherwise silent basement for several seconds as I thought, but I wasn't about to let a ton and a half of customer sludge defeat me, nor was I going to remove it one handful and one bone at a time. Ribs and collar bones detached just as readily as the others, and my arms weren't long enough to reach a pelvis, even when shoulder deep in goo. I finally figured out the answer wasn't what was inside the jumpsuits, it was the jumpsuits themselves. When I grabbed one I could pull it and its contents out simultaneously, but even that was a double edged sword. The sludge they were covered with was incredibly greasy which allowed them to slip by the others when I could grab one, but getting a good grip was almost impossible. When one would finally pop out I'd let it drop onto the conveyor belt then Skull Crusher and I would kind of bounce it into a waiting wheelbarrow which required a certain amount of timing and coordination. Then we'd cut away the clothing to expose the partially digested, bubbling, gurgling, multi-colored mess inside—yellowish fat sludge, maroon heart and liver sludge, beige and brown intestine sludge, white lung sludge, plus various other colored sludges that had been organs I couldn't identify, all with different viscosities, competing to see which could ooze out of or into the rib cage and around the pelvis furthest before splashing onto some increasingly small part of me that hadn't been spattered yet as we tried to pull the jumpsuit out of the barrow while leaving the mess in it—then we had to take it up to the chamber level and dump its repulsive contents next to the vat's load door—twenty times.

After getting them all up there I shoved each gooey blob in again with a push broom. I'll never forget the sounds they made hitting bottom—like giant overripe fruit falling onto a sidewalk. Even after taking my heels off and doing it barefoot for better traction I slipped and fell twice on the slime trails they left behind, and I nearly went into the vat myself pushing the last one in despite the safety rail, which I only just managed to hold onto with one greasy hand, and hanging there, legs and pelvis over the precipice as Skull Crusher tried to figure out how to brace himself and pull me out without going in himself, really did shake me. There's nothing like a near death experience to remind you that eternity is always just a heartbeat away, though it did make me appreciate how clean and civilized our chambers are compared to the possible alternatives, because had I lost my grip I probably would have drowned in the sludge, my lungs filled with chunky yogurt thick humanity, and I never asked, but I bet Skull Crusher would have just started the cycle if I had rather than trying to get my body out, which would have made for a rather ignominious end, though I think he would have had the good grace not to drop kick my skull after that had it remained intact. But I don't think he would have preserved it, given it to my husband with an explanation and condolences. He simply would have left it on the conveyor belt with the fragments of the rest of the customers I'd processed for the final stage of disposal and made a report to the bureau and let them handle the details. I was going to say it would have added insult to the injury, but it wouldn't have been insulting, as that kind of emotional response would have been against Skull Crusher's nature. It certainly would have added to the ignominy, though.

And when I finally calmed down we got to repeat the act for the other group, though I was considerably less cavalier with the broom, and more careful walking through the greasy mess than I had been before. I still wouldn't let Skull Crusher do it, though, and I did breathe a lot easier when we got the vats' lids closed and their cycles started again. I certainly couldn't hold it against the customers for only being half digested, and I'm sure they all would have rather been dissolved and flushed away cleanly rather than being seen as slabs of bubbling jelly on their journey to that liquid state, but I have to say I felt more than the usual satisfaction when I had their effluent flushed into the sewer after they were well and truly liquefied.

Problem solved? Oh, no. That left me with forty synthetic orange jumpsuits with 'prisoner' and a state detention center's name emblazoned on them front and back cut to rags that looked like they'd been used to clean the floors of an abattoir for a week. They weren't exactly bloody, but were sopping wet with organic and unpleasant things that would have attracted attention even in small quantities. I couldn't just throw them in the trash in case some dumpster diver found them and told the media, something the reformers wouldn't have wanted to have to explain away. I was tempted to just dump them on the detention center's front steps with a condescendingly polite note suggesting the customers be clad in natural fiber fabric in the future as specified, but that wouldn't have been professional, so I stuffed them in plastic garbage bags and drove them to the last processing center in the region with a cremation furnace and they were able to incinerate them for me as a professional courtesy.

But, by far, the worst part of the day was getting home, almost four hours late, muscles sore from moving forty headless half dissolved customers, and though I'd cleaned myself as best as I could in the bathroom at work I was streaked with partially dried sludge literally from my face to my toes, and my loving husband, who knows better than anyone the pride I take in the image I project, took one look at me, removed the pocket square from his breast pocket, wiped a generous wad of still gelatinous yellowish brown material from my hair that made me look like I was some kind of fiend who literally wallowed in her kills, examined it with some considerable disgust, folded it in said square, and handed it to me as he casually suggested that if I was going to mud wrestle on my lunch break I should strip to my underwear first like the pros.

I came so close to hitting him. I came so close to bursting into tears. I already felt like a rank amateur when I turned over the bagged jumpsuits, not just because I needed the help, but I only knew the facility's manager by reputation, and as I stood there, filthy, trying to explain what happened and appear grateful, he spent most of the time staring at my hair, and now I knew he was looking at that not so little gob of fatty sludge shed by one of my customers that I had no idea was there, and the man I loved had turned it into a joke, and he knew what I'd been through. I'd called and told him all so he wouldn't worry about my being late, and I think he was only trying to lighten the mood, and he did have a hot bath with double bath beads waiting for me, and he did have a nice hot takeout curry in the oven waiting for us after that—but he still didn't get any that night, not that I think he wanted it after he looked in that handkerchief. I had to throw out my dress, a very nice dress I might add, and my shoes which had my footprints in mottled brown on the nice white satin linings. It took me days to feel clean again after that, and the sensation of half liquefied fat and intestines squishing between your toes is something I don't recommend to anyone, and trust me—it will ruin your pedicure.

I can laugh about it now, but at the time it was seriously not funny. I called the director of the Processing and Disposal Bureau at home that night and told him what had happened, sans the marital discord. The next morning the facility, which even after our best efforts was still pretty nasty, had been steam cleaned and was spotless top to bottom. We could have used it as it was. The mess had been confined to the 'backstage' area and arriving customers would have seen nothing to cause undo distress, but it is nice to have everything shiny and clean. We also had a new wheelbarrow and push broom, and there was the biggest mixed bouquet I'd ever seen with my name on it, and a personal thank you card from the director, and by far the best part was that the customers started arriving wearing only their harnesses to ensure we never had a problem like that again, which also made it far easier to check on their satisfaction level after. I was so happy I put a flower in each of the female customers' hair before processing them that day, carefully choosing one that complimented their body type and skin tone, which I thought made them look quite elegant for their big event, though none of them seemed to appreciate it even after I told them how pretty they were. I even let them keep them for their trip through the vats so they could be blended with something beautiful, but there were still plenty of flowers to take home with me after work, one of which

I pressed in a book. The detention centers like the new system, too. They get to reuse detainee clothing, not worry about what it's made of, and naked prisoners are self-conscious and feel vulnerable, so the harnessing teams can work faster. I'll call that one win-win-win. I don't think the customers appreciate it, but I'll tally anything that speeds their journey through the system a victory for them, too. But the biggest time saver, by far, was the realization that with the harnesses resting directly against customers' skin we could redesign them to incorporate heart rate monitors and know for certain when they had expired. Before we used to wait half an hour after the last sounds in the chamber to be sure the customers were well and truly in cardiac arrest, and even then there were stories of customers reviving in vats, and horrible screams coming from them as they drowned in the caustic solution dissolving them, and while I like to think of those as spook stories told to each other by trainees, I've seen holdouts last nearly that long, so I'm not so sure. Luckily, with the HRMs we know for certain when the last heart has stopped and only need to wait minutes to be sure there are no spontaneous restarts.

I survey the chalk white material on the taut conveyor belt. All is good. On it, quite close to the bottom of the vat, amongst the last material out of it, I see the front of a broken skull and pick it up. Half of the forehead is there and both eye orbits are unbroken, but every bit of the thin bone that would have separated the eyes from the brain is gone, broken by the vat's

152

pressurization, its last remnants eroded away by the friction of the other material rubbing against it after the back of the skull came off.

"Do you think that's him?" Sunny asks as I study it —she knows me so well it's scary.

I turn it carefully in my hands several times. "It's the right size, and since he was near the top this is about where anything left of him should be." I raise it to my face like a carnival mask and look down at my pale toes with their gleaming black nails, trying to see myself the way my curious boy did, "Maybe... I hope so," I say, wiggling them, smiling. I raise my head and look at Sunny through his eye orbits. "Two hours ago he thought today would be like any other. His sentence was something amorphous, unfathomable," I tell her.

"I'm glad you were able to make it real for him."

"You know, when we were eating lunch I thought about the vat's progress with him, pictured his skeleton getting tangled together with the No Fear lady's, imagined them swirling together in the vortex, then slowly wrenching each other apart as they broke down. Is that wrong?"

"No, that's sweet, romantic even, and more intimate than anything they could have done in life, but that," she says, pointing to the bone half mask, "that's beautiful, a perfect result. It would look great in a shadow-box."

I lower the artifact and examine it minutely, and it is tempting to keep a little piece of what his face was stretched over in life, see its wide eye sockets forever not looking at me from my curio cabinet, or maybe even reinforce it with clear resin, add straps, and wear it to a masquerade among guests who would never suspect it was real. "It was more exciting for him than me," I say. "Do you want it?"

"It would only be appropriate for you—your victory, not mine."

"Ours," I tell her.

"I just blow the bubbles. You pop 'em. You pop 'em so good."

"Then why did you take that picture of his passion?" I ask, the question as leading as a carrot on a stick.

"To document his failure, of course," Sunny replies innocently, pulling out her phone, showing me the picture which is somehow even more repulsive and impressive than the reality it documents. "That's what I take pics of, always—that's what I want to remember, the biggest failures of the biggest losers sent to us, the devastating defeats that happen right here that justify their nonexistence all by themselves. Otherwise, they'd be forgotten; some things shouldn't be forgotten."

"That doesn't exactly look like failure to me," I tell her, trying not to sound too proud.

"For you, no, but for him? Crushing, because he couldn't get it into you—a treasure ship on a reef, its precious cargo scattered by storm driven waves, and you are that storm. Poor fool couldn't even get it into that tattooed old skank expiring excited in front of him, as close to him as his own skin, never had a chance. I'm sure he faded away knowing how pointless his efforts

154

were, how pointless he was, and that's sad and pathetic, but it's also true, and the truth is always beautiful."

"And the other two?" I ask.

"Her skankness?" Sunny asks, scrolling to the closeup picture of the tattooed woman's swelling sex, made even more desperate by the algorithms in digital cameras that enhance colors. "Seriously wasted passion, wanted the warmth, the hot breath in the night, but would have settled for a penis, any penis, and hated herself for not getting it. And Preggo?" She scrolls to the image of the pregnant woman so pink and shiny. "The final act in today's passion play, she came so close, and in such a pretty package—a princess with a tiny princess inside, living nesting dolls, but in the end, supply in excess of demand, order canceled, and away to the scrapyard with them," she tells me, looking down to the broken white fragments on the conveyor belt, "and the bards will curse their memory in song when they learn there was no sparkling magic bestowed by a fairy godmother inside them, that it turns out they were fashioned entirely of waste."

Sunny really is a ray of light, and she's left me speechless.

After a few moments of awkward silence she adds, "Failure is mediocrity given wing... its highest achievement."

"Show me that first picture again," I say, and she scrolls back to the No Fear tattoo wavy under its coagulating translucid deposit; then I look down to the calcium echo so fragile in my hands, turning it once more.

It breaks into three pieces when I toss it back onto the conveyor belt.

"But you are taking him home, I can tell," Sunny tells me with that knowing mind reader look of hers, and ever ready, she hands me a towel to wipe the fine white film that coats everything that comes out of those vats from my hands so I don't get any on my pretty black dress.

"Bag group two," I instruct her calmly.

She starts the machinery with a contented little smile and the still wet material moves up the conveyor belt slowly where most of the water is blown off by a pair of high velocity industrial air curtains before dropping into the grinder which reduces any last vestige of our customers still identifiable as human to a powdery paste, and in that transformation they go from waste to something that again has value. It's mixed with powdered lignin before being forced through an extruder under enough pressure to melt it and bind the loose calcium phosphate into solid five millimeter pellets which will dissolve slowly in moist soil. Finally, the machine fills and heat seals them in twenty pound bags, filling five before its hopper is empty. They're printed with the labeling of a large commercial fertilizer company that produces an indistinguishable product via the same process from what's left after animals are butchered at slaughterhouses. When we have a few pallets they're slipped into the company's distribution stream.

It gets product for free, though we tell them it's generated from unwanted pets at animal shelters. We don't have to pay to have the material landfilled. Those in power get to have people with opposing viewpoints vanish so they're not constantly wasting their time justifying their own positions instead of just getting on with making things better, and without annoying reminders that anyone ever disagreed with them. Even the processed customers get to serve their community by making gardens grow, which is probably the last thing they imagined themselves doing when they woke up this morning—win-win-win-win.

"How many do you want?" Sunny asks.

"Just one," I tell her, "I don't need every bit of him."

"There's probably more of him in this one than any other," she tells me, picking up the last bag out of the machine and carrying it to my car, putting it in the trunk for me.

"What time is the last transport?" I ask, wondering how long we have to prepare for its arrival.

"Canceled, some kind of scheduling snafu, but we'll get an extra one tomorrow."

"Then it's an early day for us," I tell her, "and forty people just had the luckiest day of their lives and will never know it."

"Especially after tomorrow," Sunny jokes, and I can't help but smile. She has such a wicked sense of humor.

As Sunny is sealing the remnants of group one in their bags I call the bureau and confirm that we'll be getting what should have been today's last two groups bright and early tomorrow morning, and probably working a couple of hours late to get all those already scheduled processed, but I don't mind. I like to work, and I'm not the only one. Sunny volunteers to clean the chambers for me, something I normally do while she's at the detention center getting our next customers, and while I usually settle for a pass with a mop dampened with a water-bleach mix followed by two passes with a dry mop, I leave her on her knees barefoot inside chamber two, her boots neatly paired outside so they don't leave any scuff marks. She's happily removing every last drip and smudge with the metal polish and microfiber cloths so the chamber will gleam for tomorrow's arrivals. The bureau's guidelines suggest, short of any actual accidents, weekly cleanings, and we used to follow them, but after the prisoners stopped arriving in their uniforms it wasn't enough, not nearly. By Fridays there were dull mottled lines down the centers of the chambers' floors, the aggregate of many hundreds of drops of biological material shed by the week's customers, and what I really didn't like was a certain subtle, stale biological odor coming from them redolent, I imagine, of poorly ventilated brothels at closing time, noticeable even when inspecting the chambers prior to loading. When I'd go inside to clean them it was quite strong, so I can only imagine what it was like for the customers when the doors were closed and sealed. Still, those arriving later in the week didn't seem to react any differently than those near the start, but I think making them shine for every new group, and ensuring any unavoidable odors are fresh, shows a level of conscientiousness and professionalism they deserve. Like I said, I am protective of my customers, and want them to have experiences, even if they find them unpleasant, that would be memorable if they were capable of memories when I'm finished with them.

As I'm walking to my car I pass the nearly half dumpster sized bin with the personal effects of those who were processed today. The bus driver deposits them there as we're doing the offload. The bureau keeps their wallets, phones, and jewelry to help offset operating costs, but by ancient tradition the executioner gets the clothing. In the middle ages it was quite valuable, as clothes worn by someone put to death were supposed to bring good luck, and even if they didn't, it's hard to imagine them bringing worse luck than their original owners had. Today they're just old clothes. Each customer's is in a clear plastic heat sealed bag with paperwork showing their name, prisoner number, execution date, and photograph stapled to the outside. Normally I deal with it at the end of the week—open the packages, get rid of the overwrap and paperwork, and donate the clothes to a charity, anonymously, of course, because their organizers might feel conflicted about where it came from, and if they took any kind of public stance against it, might end up the newest donors, and I'm trying to help the needy here, not hustling for work—because there's plenty of work, enough to keep me busy until I'm a very old lady even with the bureau's plans to open new facilities nearly weekly for the foreseeable future. As for the clothes, I usually only keep underwear for myself, but only if it's nearly new, best quality, and to my taste. It makes me feel like a boss watching the new customers arriving while wearing one of their predecessor's panties, and sometimes I play a little game with myself where I try to determine, just by looking at them suspended naked before me, whether any will have been arrested wearing something better than what I have on. If I see a likely candidate I'll signal Sunny who'll snap a picture of her, and then we'll check after work. I'm not very good at it. The most sophisticated looking ladies sometimes get taken in the most atrocious, stretched elastic, mom briefs.

A patch of deep, nearly luminescent, electric blue at the top of the bin catches my eye. I pick it up and turn it over a few times in my hands and see that it's either a swimsuit or leotard in a bag all by itself, which means it was the only thing the woman who wore it had on when she was arrested, which is a bit strange. The police'll take people anywhere they can find them, but it's not normal to have them pluck someone out of a pool or from a dance studio. I glance at the paperwork, and the attached picture is a bit surprising. It belonged to the well worn tattooed woman immediately ahead of my curious boy, the one who intercepted his passion so assiduously, the one who bloomed for me so beautifully, and the one with plastic eyes nearly as bright as this fabric, which probably lured many a gullible guy into torrid one night encounters before she cut them loose for some imperfection they didn't know they had. I tear the bag open. It's a leotard, and ruined, which is a shame because it looks quite pricey. Its front is highly abraded and dust stained, a few small blood smears mark the high cut right leg opening, so they must have taken her none too gently, and that makes me smile. I wouldn't want to think of her actually getting abused, but she looked like she would have benefited from a little manhandling once in a while. I hold the garment to my nose, close my eyes, and inhale deeply. After weeks in that bag it still smells so strongly of sweat and failure that it makes me weak, so I take another whiff, longer and deeper. Then I toss the paperwork and bag, and take the little garment with me —that I have use for.

Part III

I'm home early, and having had a perfect work day it's time to make preparations for a special night. I go to the bedroom, hang my nice dress up, put my shoes away, drop my underwear in the hamper, splash on some perfume, then, quite naked, touch up my hair and switch from empathetic pink to fuck me red lipstick before turning my attention to my sizzling blue prize. There's more than enough time to hand wash it and let it air dry before my husband gets home. That's not what I want, though. I step into it slowly and luxuriate in the feeling of the cool silky fabric stretching over my skin, certain it'll bring me the luck that eluded its previous owner as I slip into its quarter length sleeves that her fleshy upper arms needed, but mine don't, and adjust it to my body, the process a bit like stuffing a sausage. The fit is perfect, and it makes me feel filthy, physically filthy, and if I stand still and inhale through my nose deeply I can just catch the dead woman's odor which sends a little tingling thrill up my spine.

I take in my reflection in the full length mirror. The bedraggled polyester makes it look like I lost a full body belt sander duel. Its frayed surface is, if anything, more opaque than the undamaged portions, yet if I look carefully I can still see the contours of my nipples through it. I try to picture what No Fear looked like in it. I'm sure her spray tan legs looked a lot more sophisticated than my full moon white examples do protruding from the leg holes rather shockingly, but my husband says he likes their ghostly look, and she doesn't have legs anymore, or anything else, so I win, but it does highlight exactly how short a straw I drew when they were handing out the melanin. Even so, I can't say the look isn't enticing in its own way, and as I turn I like the way it exposes just enough of my ass cheeks to make it look like maybe I'm a dancer and it rode up during ballet practice and I didn't notice—sexy, but not overtly slutty.

My husband won't be home for well over an hour, so I start dinner, and think about him running his eyes over me like my curious boy did, though he'll see a lot more when he does, and have infinitely more options. I put the hot things in a warm oven. I put the prepared produce in the cold refrigerator. I turn on some smooth jazz and pose on the couch like a modern realist painter's take on a portrait odalisque from a nineteenth century Paris salon, prepared to just wait there until my man gets home to ravage me. I manage about five minutes before I begin touching myself through the taut smooth fabric gently, another five before I push the damp crotch aside with one hand and let the fingers of the other find the sweet spot.

Honestly, I'm only planning on warming myself up, but soon I'm rubbing myself earnestly. I come close to getting up and getting my favorite dildo, but no, I decide, nothing inside me until he is, and three minutes later I'm trembling in orgasm. "You bitch, you bitch, you bitch," I growl until it fades, unsure whether I'm calling the woman making me come a bitch for bringing me off like such a whore, or calling the woman unashamedly coming a bitch for being such an unrepentant pervert. Either way the effort leaves me panting and exhausted, so exhausted I do it again.

"It looks like you started the party without me."

I jerk awake from a sound sleep confused by the words before I realize they're my husband's, then hastily rearrange the leotard's crotch and my legs to a more ladylike condition, not that I'd have objected if he'd awakened me the way Prince Charming probably did with Sleeping Beauty before it was cleaned up for the fairy-tale, but he's a bit too proper for that, too much of a gentleman to understand that I love him so much he can have me any time, any way, conscious or not, but I know he loves me in his own way, and I love him for that.

"Wow, you were really out."

"I was thinking of you," I stammer, lying. I had been thinking about him, but just before I was overwhelmed I thought of my curious boy's ass, which I stared at unapologetically as he slid into the chamber until he was occluded by the long legged woman entering behind him. It's not that I wanted him, but I wanted him to want me, wanted him to die for me, and he did, so beautifully, and exactly how I wanted, pleasure and profession fusing perfectly at that moment.

Suddenly aware of the stickiness between my thighs and on my fingers, and horrified I might look like one of the spent ladies fresh from processing, I dart to the little bathroom, close and lock the door behind me, and hurriedly moisten one of the fancy hand towels we put out for guests and wipe myself clean.

"You can think about anyone you like," my beautiful man tells me through the door without even trying the knob, seeing all the way through my lie as I imagine him casually leaning against the wall, jacket slung over his shoulder, one leg jauntily lifted, foot against the jamb. He's never stood like that in his life, but his smooth low voice evokes that kind of vision, that kind of feeling. "Like I've been telling you, do anything you want with them, so long as you don't kiss them while you're doing it, and have the good manners to turn them to sludge and wash them down the drain when you're done," he jokes.

Like Sunny, he knows me too damn well, can read me like a large print book. God, I love him. "You know

I always do," I tell him.

"And one day you can show me. I think you need to institute a take your husband to work day."

"No," I say. "I'll tell you anything. I'll tell you everything... but I wouldn't want that." Most people who work in processing facilities hide what they do from their families, and the bureau provides cover stories, phone numbers to benign sounding dummy companies answered like they're real businesses, and other deceptions for those who feel reality is too heavy a burden for their loved ones, but I've always been honest about my profession with him, even the details, and I'm glad. I'm proud of what I do, and would have had to have myself hosed down with cold water at the facility instead of getting a hot bath with double beads after the jumpsuit incident if I hadn't shared that part of my life with him. There's no rule that says immediate family can't know, but I haven't sugar coated it, either —if he tells anyone his life will be forfeit for sure, mine endangered.

"Don't want me to learn all your secrets?" he teases.

"No," I snap. "Yes, I mean... I tried to wait." I turn the towel wrong side out and hang it back on the bar, "And I've never actually touched a customer. Why would I when I can touch you?" But as soon as the words are out of my mouth I realize that I had, in fact, touched my curious boy, the only one ever, not counting post processing inspections which don't count, and the jumpsuit incident, but I can't imagine him being jealous of anyone without a pulse—or a head, or skin. I fix my hair as best I can and look at myself in the mirror. I decide I don't look as spent as all that and open the door.

"And just what are you wearing?" he asks, looking me up and down.

"A dead woman's very last possession."

"You didn't?"

"Just before lunch."

"Who was she?"

"A frightened little nobody who desperately wanted to live. Now she's just nobody."

"Please tell me you washed it."

"Does it look like I washed it?" I ask, inching towards him. "Does it smell like I washed it?"

He runs a finger over the skin of my chest just above the yellow piping at the garment's top before grabbing the leotard by the fabric at the neck hole. He pulls it away from my body and twists, but doesn't even lean in to take a peek at my breasts, the look on his face more disdain than arousal. Then he turns and tugs me along behind him into the garage where he points to the new sack of pellets I've put with the others next to the gardening things. "I take it Little Miss Nobody is carefully bagged up there and looking forward to seeing the garden," he says, pointing.

I shake my head, though technically she is probably mostly in there. Being just ahead of my curious boy what was left of her bones would have been well mixed with his during grinding, and bound together in varying proportions pellet to pellet as they were extruded, but she was far too unimportant to be honored with a place on the fertilizer pile on her own merit, and no matter how much it inspires my husband tonight, her leotard will be in the trash tomorrow, still unwashed.

"Then who?"

"I'll tell you later."

"Somebody famous?" he asks.

"No," I tell him, but I see why he asked—a popular singer of overproduced pop who thought she could hide a message between the lines of a song that was instantly suppressed, a gorgeous A-list actor who turned down the wrong role when he failed to realize that even that can look like rebellion, and two politicians, one suspected of more than they could prove, so they accused him of more than he could have done, and another who fanatically supported the reforms, so probably never imagined he'd get such a close look at them in practice, and a dozen other national and local celebrities have come home with me the same way, and whose names I've carefully written on their bags, and whose slow release into my garden's soil is making it the envy of the neighborhood.

"Somebody you knew?"

I also brought home one of my high school teachers, a favorite who always encouraged me to follow my dreams. I think she thought I was going to save her when we made eye contact before I had her group loaded into their chamber, but I just thanked her for believing in me and followed my dream. Rather sadly, I also brought home a neighbor's son who ended up at my facility when she thought he was away at university. I gave her the sack of pellets before she found out about his arrest, sentence, and its execution, and for the life of me I can't imagine what he did that would have gotten him fast tracked like that. I mean, if you go to the wrong protest or make an ill advised social media post it's normally at least a month or two between that and when you meet someone like me. The reformers want to give the illusion that justice is as considered as it is unavoidable, that predetermined outcomes aren't preordained.

But for the families of people who run afoul of the reforms the insult to the injury is not getting a body back for rites, but there are far too many of them to keep the numbers from sinking into the public consciousness, so they're told they've been buried in unmarked graves as per regulations, and in a way it's true, and if nobody sees those graves there can't be that many of them. Naturally, I didn't tell the neighbor exactly what was in the bag—if I did it might have cost both our lives, and looked like cruel boasting. As far as she, or any of our other neighbors know, I work at a fertilizer plant that specializes in animal based products, and in a way that's also true, with me just bringing her a sample bag as a neighborly gesture a few days before she received some terrible news, but the pellets really did perk up her garden when she got around to using them; they're a good product, so— lemons to lemonade, and she has asked for, and gotten, a couple of more bags—no relation.

"Nope," I tell my dear hubby about the bag he's curious about containing my curious boy, "I never saw him before."

"There's no name on the bag."

"That's because I never asked it."

"Intriguing," he says, raising an eyebrow.

"I'll tell you later. Dinner's ready. Or you can bend me over those bags, take me from behind right now, and I'll tell you everything while you're inside me."

"You're such a little ghoul," he tells me playfully, yanking the leotard up into my butt crack to fully expose my cheeks and giving me a not so playful slap on the ass, propelling me into the kitchen with a pink hand print on it; he always comes home hungrier than he is horny, and enjoys making me wait no matter how much I need him.

"I take it, it was a good day," he says as I assemble the BLTs.

"The best," I tell him, smiling.

"You always say that."

"It really was."

"How many?"

"Only two transports, so we finished a bit early."

"But they were full?"

I nod. They always are these days.

"You're such a good girl, too."

"I am."

"And the new bag?"

"Not right now."

"And you're such a little tease," he tells me.

"Oh, I'm definitely that," I say, thinking about my curious boy looking at my slowly rolling hips as I had him shuttled to his chamber.

When we've finished our sandwiches I wash the dishes like a good little nineteen-fifties housewife while my attentive husband fondles me slowly from behind, making me feel incredibly barefoot and short as he does, and appreciate just how thin the fabric of No Fear's little leotard is as he presses his erection against my lower back through the soft wool of his office trousers. I rise to my toes and rub my ass against him, trying to force his hand. I just want him to grab a knife from the block and slit the dirty polyester from my shoulder-blades to my crotch and jam his way into whatever hole he finds first while I scrub the dishes. I save the pan with the congealed bacon grease for last in case I can tempt him into taking the tightest plunge and he wants to lube me up with a twisting finger-full first, but he makes no move to mount me, because he doesn't have to hurry. He already has my soul, or the network of connected neurons that will have to serve as one until something better comes along, which means he can have my body whenever he pleases, any way he pleases. I'm as helpless with him as my customers are with me, and he likes order at home even when I crave the release of chaos. When everything's dried and neatly stacked he turns me to him and I can finally see the lust kindling in his eyes.

I turn and envelop him in my arms. "Make me do something disgusting," I tell him.

171

"You've already managed that," he replies, stepping back and pulling the front of the leotard away from my body, but this time tilting his head to get a good long look at my tits, at my stiffening pink nipples, then lowering his nose and taking a deep whiff of the mixed odors he finds there before letting it snap back with that distinctive 'thwack' sound polyester makes.

"Please," I beg, "I want it to be so twisted I won't be able to look in a mirror for a week."

His eyes twinkle.

"No, not that," I say, as he spins me, then yanks the leotard down to my waist, trapping my arms at my sides, twisting the fabric tightly at my back so I can't squirm free, then quick marching me down the hall bare chested, breasts bouncing, using much more force than's necessary. When he gets me into the bedroom he jerks the garment down to my ankles and pushes me hard so I stumble onto the bed naked except for my lipstick, nail polish, and wedding ring.

I start to feel real dread as he undresses, and instinctively pull my calves beneath me and cover my breasts. I know what's coming and think about making a break for it, but know he'll grab me before I get both feet on the floor if I do. "Oh, no, no... no," I tell him, "not missionary under the covers. You're not going to do me like some middle aged soccer mom who volunteers for everything except an interesting sex life," and the flash of blue on the floor seems to mock me when I realize this was probably its owner's idea of paradise, and may have even been her reality time and again until I snuffed it out for her, something I won't be able to do for myself in the next few minutes barring a miracle. "Bring the new bag in here, empty it on the bed, push me face down in the pellets and take me hard. Throw me on the carpet, bend my legs back, and pile drive me into the floor. Turn on the game, force yourself into my mouth and come down my throat when your team scores..."

Before I can make another suggestion my man is on top of me, has the comforter over us, the lights out. The truth, of course, is that I'm not afraid of boring banalities, of being unsatisfied and unsatiated, but hate that my dear husband can make mounting me like a Bible belt preacher as exciting as my customers find a trip through my chambers, keeping in mind that excitement has anticipation, stimulation, and reaction, and my reaction is as strong as any of theirs, as embarrassing in the circumstance, but stops short of the blissful unconsciousness they get when it's over. It's not as humiliating if it's something bizarre, if I can blame a kink for how I reacted. I brought a harness home from work and he's strapped me into it, hung me from the rafters in the garage, blindfolded me, and fucked me until I was a babbling mess, and when he was finished he held a ball vibrator against my oozing sex and made me come until I cried and begged him to let me down or kill me, but he'll only do that for me on my birthday and Easter no matter how much I beg, and I've gotten to the point that I welcome getting older just so I can feel him tightening those straps before he

173

plunges into me. But most of the time I find myself in our bed, on my back, naked, clinging desperately to him as he services me, wishing I didn't love it so much.

"No, please..." I beg, "not like this... not like this," and I mean it, but my sex is embarrassingly wet, so wet that the fleshy parts of my inner thighs are as slick as my depths, and my legs have already spread of their own accord. Ever the gentleman, my husband reaches down and tests my readiness with a practiced finger, inserting it first one knuckle deep, then two, and everything being to his satisfaction, slides his penis into me with unneeded restraint, filling and stretching me simultaneously, forcing a gasp from my lips. He pins my wrists next to my head so I don't attempt escape, and begins taking long, slow, machine-like strokes, and I instantly surrender to the feeling of being filled, close my eyes, lie back and let him have me, concentrating on the pleasure and the humiliation of being taken like this, as he does something to me that thousands of uninspired women who've never done anything to change the world are experiencing right now, women no better than a herd of wide eyed cows being serviced in the breeding shed when you think about it.

"Have you calmed down, young lady?" he asks after twenty or thirty strokes.

"You know I don't like to be calmed like this," I complain.

"But I like to do it. Excitable fillies need a firm hand."

"You know I'm yours," I tell him. "You can do

anything to me."

"And I'm doing this."

"I fucking love you, you bastard."

"Not as much as I love fucking you."

"I fucking love you," I sigh, repeating myself.

At the bottom of every stroke he starts asking, "Who's my *femme fatale*?"

If I don't answer, "I am," before he gets to the top of the next one he pauses, so I end up repeating, "I am, I am, I am," over and over as he asks, but this isn't the kind of embarrassment I crave. It would be so much more degrading if he'd use, 'Who's your Daddy?'

After answering him twenty-five or thirty times he's satisfied and asks, "What got you so worked up that you had to start without me?" as he continues pumping me with measured strokes.

"I met someone at work today, a curious boy," I tell him.

"Oh, how nice."

"It was... refreshing."

"New intern?"

"No, customer. He really took an interest, you know? Plenty try to avoid the chamber, or just buy a minute or two more, but he wanted to know things. He really wanted to know things."

"What did you do?"

"I processed him."

"I bet you enjoyed that." He always knows exactly what to say. He starts to increase the speed of his thrusts.

"I did. I really did, and he was no trouble."

"I bet he wasn't."—exactly what to say.

"Did you make him beg?"

"They all beg... his group got a little feisty at the start, but I took care of them."

"You always do."—exactly what to say.

"He even thanked me... twice. I've never had a customer thank me before."

"I'm glad. I'm sure most of them recognize your talent, but are too nervous or shy to say anything."— exactly what to say.

I'm getting closer.

"And after? Did you look?"

"Oh, I looked."

"And? Was he a satisfied customer?"

"He was probably the most satisfied customer I've ever had," I tell him proudly.

We're both breathing harder now. I struggle again— but this time it's not to get free, but to prove to myself I can't.

"They always melt for you."—exactly what to say.

"You know, I think I heard his... exclamation of satisfaction."

"From outside?" hubby asks.

"While I was increasing the gas level. It was amazing... pathetic and passionate... failure's fleeting swansong."

"Heart breaker."—exactly what to say.

"It shocked poor Sunny. She was just standing there... wide eyed, mouth open."

"And did it shock you?"

"It made me giggle. Executioners aren't supposed to giggle, especially while carrying out a sentence."

"I'm so glad he gave it up for you so dramatically."—exactly what to say.

"Then, when we took them out and looked... poor Sunny was crestfallen."

"I thought he was the most satisfied customer you ever had?"

"It wasn't the satisfaction. It was what left it. I think she was expecting something magnificent. What we found was ravening, pugnacious, even, but frankly, pathetic... with this funny little up curve near the tip— no better than a supermarket sausage, eight to a pack on a little tray covered with cling film at the meat counter."

"And I would have loved to hear you whisper that into his dead ear."—exactly what to say.

Two or three powerful strokes shoves me closer with a lurch. My breath is getting ragged and I'm having a hard time concentrating, but my words are only slightly clipped when I manage to ask, "But who am I to complain? The poor guy had to go through life with it, and even in death he left two women shaking their heads."

"Well, I'm glad you brought that naughty curious boy's misshapen reign of terror to an end."

"Yes," I say, gasping, "and straight into the vat with him after that."

"So after he melted for you," my husband says, his

voice still warm and smooth, "you made him melt for you again."

"While Sunny and I ate noodles, then it was down the drain and away to the wastewater treatment plant."

"I bet he didn't expect that." There's another subtle increase in the speed of his thrusts.

"They never do."

"That's my girl."—exactly what to say.

"And what's left... is in the bag you found, with the leftovers of a few of those closest to him, in the literal sense."

"I'm so proud of you," he tells me, tension in his voice this time. He releases my wrists, drops the full weight of his torso onto mine, making my soft flesh conform to his as he wraps his arms around me, gripping an ass cheek in each hand as he does for better control. "I don't tell you often enough, but I am."— exactly what to say.

"He was just flesh and bone in the end, like all men... until he wasn't," I tell him.

Much, much closer—I hold my breath, press my eyes closed as hard as I can, blackening my already dark world. His penis increases speed until it's like a runaway piston in some eternal machine. This time I'm going to do it. This time I'm going to hold my breath until I pass out. This time I'm going to know what it's like. The wait is unendurable. The pleasure builds as my need for air grows. The horror of my submission crashes to the front of my psyche again as I try not to breathe. "Not like this," I manage to beg, clinging to

178

my wonderful husband with arms and legs, fists clenched, but unable to stop him, unable to slow him. I want him to have me so badly, but I don't want what's coming. "Not like this," I beg. "It can't be like this." My lungs are empty and I have to struggle to keep from taking a breath. I press my lips together and my head thrashes from side to side. I can't tell him it can't be like this again, but it can't be like this.

Our orgasms hit simultaneously, like a pair of tsunamis crashing together in the open ocean creating a shockwave felt around the world but seen by no one, a primal eruption against my twitching cervix, half proclamation of conquest by rite, half celebration of life, both unendurable. I scream through closed lips in surrender and disbelief, desperate to feel oblivion overtake me—not forever, just for a while. I need to know what the end is like. But I can't control my body. It sucks in a deep breath of cool clean air at the crescendo that makes me feel so alive, and another, and another. We lie motionless, panting in the dark. A minute later my husband pulls his softening penis from my body and rolls off of me, keeping a widely flexed hand against my flesh at all times, and I breathe. I breathe and breathe and breathe, eyes closed.

"Did you manage it this time?" he asks.

"No," I tell him, taking deep breaths, satiating myself with air. "My customers do, but I never can."

"They have help, help from the best. They're so lucky to meet you. Any idiot can turn on the gas and snuff them out, but you make them sweat. You make

179

them do the eternal dance. You make them know what it's like to feel alive, maybe for the first time, and maybe for just seconds, but you make them feel something before they feel nothing, so the approaching void becomes truly terrifying. And for that they must be genuinely grateful as they feel themselves flickering out."

"You always know exactly what to say," I tell him out loud, basking in the afterglow.

A few minutes later he idly quotes me, "He was just flesh and bone in the end, like all men."

"I've never found anything else."

"Is that all I am?"

"Now?" I sigh, then pause to reflect, "Yes."

"That's what we all fear, isn't it?"

"Why should we fear the truth?" I ask, but my heart isn't in it.

"But—what if it *was* me?"

"You?"

"Yes, what if it was really me? What if I vanished one day then showed up at your facility for processing? The door opens and there I am harnessed and waiting with the rest. Have you ever thought about that?"

"Oh, yes," I tell him with too much relief in my voice. I didn't think he'd ever bring it up, "you don't know how many times."

"Seriously?"

"Yes."

"Why didn't you tell me?"

"Because all choice would have been taken from

you before you got there, all decisions made."

"And?"

"And what?"

"Would you process me?" my dear husband asks, voice tightening.

"You don't want to know."

"I do."

"Are you sure?" I ask.

"Would you?"

"Absolutely I would."

After a moment he asks, "No hesitation?"

"None, then you'd get a standard disposal."

"Dissolved?"

"Dissolved, flushed away, bone fragments ground and pelletized with the rest."

"Let's make a deal," he tells me with a forced smile I can't see in the dark but know is there, "you can... you can make me dance for you, and all the rest that goes with it in that box, but you can't turn me into goo. I really, really don't want to be goo."

"My curious boy didn't want that, either. He even asked about it. It didn't help him. It wouldn't help you."

"You're not serious..." he says, giving my hand a little squeeze I don't return, "Please?"

"I'm not teasing you. This isn't pillow talk. You brought it up. I have thought about it. I've made decisions. With the way things are either one of us could get arrested tomorrow and never know why, and with my position, and you being married to someone in my position, we'd be fast tracked, trials complete and sentences passed before we were even taken—hours from arrest to processing, days if we're lucky, not weeks, not months. I could end up at my own facility to be processed by a newly promoted Sunny using all my tricks, or you really could show up for me."

"They'd never send me to you, though," he says.

"Yes, they would. I talked to the head of the bureau, years ago. I told him in the event it happens I want you, and he said he'd make sure of it. I made it clear I wasn't asking for it. I didn't want any misunderstanding... but if you go I get you. It's in the system."

"Why?"

"Isn't it obvious? I wouldn't want anyone else to do it."

His breath catches. This isn't romance to him, but it's what we'd be left with. "I won't go," he whispers.

"No, no," I warn. "If they come for you don't resist. Let them put the harness on you. Let whoever comes for you take you. It's not that bad if you go with them, but don't hesitate. Don't hesitate at all." I don't want the testicles I've caressed and licked in the night punctured by Sunny's electrodes no matter how persuasive they are, but most of all I don't want her to have that intimacy I saw her prod induce. I don't want him to sing her a song like an innocent child as she drains him passionlessly.

"You've thought of me... as bone fragments on a conveyor belt?"

"Many times, and if they come for you that's what

you'll be no matter what, so don't fight them."

My moody giant is silent for a bit then, resignation in his voice, says, "And then you'd bring my bag home, put it on the pile with the rest."

"No. You'd be liquid, pellets—waste. I'd leave it in the sewer, in the bags. It's a novelty to have a movie star or favorite teacher feeding the garden. It makes me smile. It makes me laugh. But if you think I'd carefully spread the little bits of you that weren't liquefied around the roses and smell their flowers every spring and remember you with sad sighs think again."

"Maybe we shouldn't be talking about this," he warns.

"Are you frightened?"

"Disturbed."

"You should be frightened."

He takes a breath. "I am, you don't know how much."

"Good, you called me a little ghoul, and that's all I am... until this sinks in. I've told you what's going to happen if you're sent to me, without platitudes, without emotion. Now, it's obvious you haven't thought about this before, and that's OK. I run into denial every day in every customer, but now that I've made you confront it, now that you know, what do you think, honestly?"

"I... I'm afraid I wouldn't be able to take it."

"That wouldn't matter. You should know that by now. Anything else?"

"Yes." My dear husband takes a deep breath. "I'm afraid I wouldn't be as brave as your curious boy."

"Brave? Is that what you think? He wasn't brave. He was terrified. He could hardly speak. He wouldn't look me in the eye, none of them do, not after they find out what I'm going to do to them, and they only learn half of it. The only thing that keeps them from trembling is shock and forcing themselves to disbelieve. Does that make you feel better?"

"No."

"And speaking of disbelief, don't pretend I'll be able to save you if it happens. I can't sneak you out the back so we can run away to somewhere where there aren't any reforms, because there isn't any place to run, because it doesn't work like that. I'm good at my job. If it comes to it you just relax and stare straight ahead and let me do it and know I'll do it well. Don't think about anything until it begins because there's nothing to think about, then think about me because there won't be anything else, ever."

"I don't want to talk about this. Please, please stop," he tells me, his discomfort level rising.

"No, you have to hear me. This is probably the most important thing—no matter how much I try to prepare you now, if it happens, it'll happen faster than you can imagine, and while speed is always humane with these things, it's never welcome when time's up. It's minutes, just minutes, from the time the bus door opens until the gas chamber door closes, and just minutes from the time that door closes until the processing is over—and you're gone; it's over, forever. I want you to really try to imagine what those minutes would be like for you."

"I am trying."

"And not even two hours until there's nothing, nothing left of you except the sticky chemicals you were made from, all mixed up with the sticky chemicals of a bunch of other unlucky people, and a few bone fragments for the grinder. It's not that I want these things to happen—I don't, desperately, but if they do I want you to know that I'll still love you, even when you're gasping and whimpering and begging me to stop... and I don't." After a few seconds I add, "That's what I needed to say. I should have told you sooner because I do think of it, and often, every time a transport backs up for unloading, if I'm honest. I steel my face and stand erect and hope I don't see you there when the doors open, and if you're not there it's like Christmas day, and if you ever are it'll be like Christmas after there's been a death in the family, but Christmas will still come; nobody can stop it..." I take a deep breath. "Is there anything else you want to know?"

"When it was over and you opened the chamber would you..." he starts, then falters.

He can't ask. I've made it too real. He thinks mentioning it is trivial now, but it's what I want to hear him say because it's the one question I can answer with certainty. Vulgar as it is in the abstract, it's the only thing left in those chambers you can associate with love, no matter how deviously it's twisted in those few breathless minutes. "Check to see if you ejaculated?" I prompt with affected dispassion.

"Yes," he whispers darkly.

"I would," I tell him, "first thing."

"Should I be grateful for that?"

"Yes." A few moments later I add, "and the one special thing I'd do for you is to make sure you were at the front of a group. I wouldn't want you rubbing up against some anonymous woman's back in your last moments. If you come it'll be against a steel door in the dark, breathless and terrified, but it will be for me alone, and it wouldn't matter if you splattered the door like an abstract expressionist or just left a pathetic little smudge, it would be perfect. You might only enjoy it for moments, or it might not even register as pleasure, but I'd have it for a lifetime, no matter how many casual boyfriends or 'til death husbands I had after you. And I'd tell every one of them exactly what you did for me, no euphemisms. And that would be the only story I ever told about you, because it would be the only one that mattered, that you died for me, twice."

The silence that follows is as black as the inside of one of my chambers. When he finally speaks it's to say, "I suppose I should thank you for that, too."

"You should, you really should," I tell him softly.

He swallows. "Thank you."

"You're welcome, now sleep."

"I have one more question. You don't have to answer it if you don't want to."

"Ask."

"It's about what happened today."

"Yes?"

"Did you put your curious boy at the front?"

186

My mood lightens instantly and my laughter reverberates off the shadowed walls. "Him?" I ask in disbelief. "Oh, no... just... no. He was interesting, different. He even had a cute little ass the harness lifted and framed perfectly, but it didn't matter to me where he was in the group as long as he got processed. I really, really wanted to process him because his thanks didn't mean anything until it was complete, and then meant even more when disposal was." I pause for a moment to collect my thoughts. "Don't get me wrong, I did want to help him understand when he asked, but only so he could appreciate what was happening, which is to say, appreciate me. I was the star performer; he was the appreciative audience, and while I was probably more grateful for his emphatic applause than the woman ahead of him, I get new audiences every day. I mean, as far as I'm concerned he was never anything more than goo for the pipes and fertilizer for the yard. His processing was the highlight of his empty life, his disposal the highlight of my full afternoon. I even waved bye-bye to him as he flowed into the sewer."

My dear husband sighs and pulls me closer to his warm, resting body and tells me, "And you always know exactly what to say, too."

I roll onto my side and drape an arm around him possessively. His body relaxes. I can feel his consciousness fading away. Soon he'll be dreaming of unyielding steel doors in black spaces, of ejaculating for me with no escape, of dying for me, and I wouldn't want it any other way, because he has no way out; he will die for me again, and again, and again, and again, and again, as I will for him—unless we get unlucky. I haven't told him everything, though, about my decisions. If he is sent to me his group will go first. I don't want him to understand it. I just want him to experience it, and if that's unfair considering what I did for a stranger then so be it, but it's what I've decided, what I want. And before that I'm going to make a last grand romantic gesture, the kind he doesn't think I'm capable of despite our love. Just before I have his group advanced into the chamber I'm going to slip my wedding band off, lubricate it with my own saliva, and shove it into his anus as deeply as I can without a word, pressing it hard against his prostate and pulsing it rhythmically until I get a reaction. It will be with him through his passion in the chamber. It will be with him in the vat until there is no more him and it drops to the bottom during the disposal cycle, some of the molecules that were a part of his body passing through its center as it falls. Then I'll retrieve it from the debris, personally, and put it on a necklace and wear it until the day I die, or the day I'm detained and they take it from me.

I close my eyes and try to think about my curious boy as something more than fertilizer, probably for the last time. If I could tell him anything I'd tell him it's not that he didn't matter, but that he didn't matter the way he thought he did. From the moment he entered my facility, long before that, actually, maybe from the moment he was born, he was just part of the effluent that drained out of that vat, inseparable from the others, and they inseparable from those drained yesterday, and the lucky ones who don't know they're lucky sleeping warm tonight and hoping and dreaming who I'll drain away tomorrow, an endless dark stream of humanity rendered down to its simplest chemistry that will keep flowing because we can't seem to find any alternative, because we can't find any way of defining ourselves as more than that. And as long as they show up they'll need my help to make that transition—from thinking, breathing beings to lifeless flesh, from lifeless flesh to peptide rich syrup, and for better or worse they'll think about me while they can; for a few minutes I'll be the most important thing in their lives, the only thing in their lives, really, and that makes me feel pretty awesome.

I don't know if I'm doing good in this world, none of us ever do. That's for the people who come after us to decide, and even then it'll probably have more to do with justifying their own actions rather than actually evaluating what led them to look back and appraise us. But whole worlds vanish because of me, snuffed out like candles between my metaphorical fingers by the actions of my actual fingers—and each time one world is extinguished a new one is born, the fruit of my labor and a customer's struggles, and that means I'm making a difference—for good, for evil, for something, maybe even for nothing, but I'm making a difference.

I take another deep breath and cuddle up to my man,

pulling myself even closer to him, basking in the afterglow, not the least bit concerned to feel our warm bodily fluids flowing out of my sex and between my cheeks and thickening, getting sticky. And I let myself sleep. Tomorrow will be a busy day.

the end

(with credit to Titivillus—for his usual contributions)

Made in United States
Troutdale, OR
08/11/2024